The Disappearance of

Darcie Malone

An
Emily Menotti
Mystery

by

MARYELLEN WINKLER

Also by Maryellen Winkler:

What Killed Rosie?

Cruising to Death

The Disappearance of Darcie Malone
Copyright 2016, Maryellen Winkler
All rights reserved.

ISBN
978-1-935751-42-7 (paperback)
978-1-935751-43-4 (eBook)

Published by
Scribbulations LLC
Kennett Square, Pennsylvania
U.S.A.

Acknowledgments

Many thanks to Aurora Cannon for her editorial
assistance, and to Ed Charlton and
Grace Spampinato for their continuing support.

Prologue

The summer night was soft on my skin. The leaves on the arching trees were silent. Beneath the glow of a street lamp, I watched a young woman exit the Laundromat with a basket of clean clothes. I leaned against Jack's car, closed my eyes, and wished for a cigarette to better inhale the beauty of the quiet night.

The air was still and heavy as if the town were under a sorcerer's spell. I was likewise in no hurry to move. Then I heard the shuffling of feet through the dry leaves on the brick path. Jack, I thought, leaving the home of the friends we'd been visiting.

Then I heard the voice. It was an old man's voice, quavering with song:

Dar-cie Ma-lone... Dar-cie Ma-lone...
Darcie, why won't you come home?

I opened my eyes. There was no one there.

Chapter One

I thought about that experience almost every waking moment for the next few days. Who was Darcie Malone? Who was the old man asking for her return? Was he her father, brother, husband? Why had she left? Was she a runaway or a murder victim? I felt an irresistible pull from her, as if her name were a mastiff dog yanking on its leash. I decided to try and find out what I could about Darcie Malone. My first stop, as everyone's is these days, was the Internet.

I went to the search engine and typed "Darcie Malone." I got a few matches for Dorothy Malone, and a slew of Maloneys, but no Darcie Malone.

At a loss for what to do next, I sat at my kitchen table and had another cup of coffee, contemplated the grass that needed cutting in the backyard, thought about the groceries I needed to purchase, and then reexamined my Darcie experience. Why did it happen to me? Did it have anything to do with where I was standing that night?

Next I got out my bike and pedaled to the Sussex County Library where I looked up local history via its only newspaper, the *Sussex Sentinel*. I was guessing that old news events had not yet been added to its computer database. Sussex County is a small, sparsely populated, underfunded area of the economically struggling state of New Hampshire. There were few enough library employees, let alone ones with the spare time to transcribe old news stories into new files.

I searched the archives for hours before finding my Darcie Malone, a young girl who had disappeared on the night of September 6, 1969, when she and her boyfriend had gone off for a midnight picnic. I had been standing across the street from her home at Ten Orchard Road, on September 6, 1999, when I heard the shuffling feet and the old man's voice singing her name.

Darcie's body was never found, but her boyfriend had shown up the next morning wandering by the Severn River. He was dazed and speechless and immediately taken to the local hospital, and later to a sanitarium. He never spoke, never wrote a note, never offered a word of explanation as to what happened that night. In 1998, at the age of forty-seven, he died in his sleep.

I had been just a few years older than Darcie in 1969 and had probably spent that weekend at an outdoor party of some kind myself, drinking and dancing with my soon-to-be (now ex-) husband.

Although it was assumed that Darcie had been the victim of a lover's quarrel, the mystery of her disappearance was never solved. Her father was sure that one day the boyfriend would regain his sanity and tell everyone what had happened. He never did. Three months after the boyfriend's death, Darcie's father died of heart failure. There was a brief mention of Darcie's brother, Albert. The boyfriend's name had been Walter Everly.

I knew of the eccentric Everly family. Everyone in town did. Some Everlys had run for public office under the Libertarian banner, some never cut their lawns and called the overgrowth a "natural garden," and some had been arrested for growing marijuana.

The newspaper articles about Darcie seemed to imply an opposite sort of family life. Her parents were referred to as "bookish" and "shy," as was she. Her father occasionally taught composition and grammar at the high school. Her mother kept house. Her brother Albert owned a hardware store. There was no mention of high jinks or scandal.

The mystery was now thirty years old. The only eyewitness, deceased. Where would I begin? I searched the *Sussex Sentinel* obituaries for Darcie's mother, Mary Malone. There were none. If I were to guess Mrs. Malone's age as about forty in 1969, she would be at least seventy now.

I located the Swansea phone book and found only one listing for a Malone, Albert, at 10 Orchard Road. The family had never moved. Perhaps they were still waiting for Darcie to come home.

I thought about Darcie and wondered where she might be. Was she lying dead somewhere, her bones uncherished and alone? Or was she hiding in some remote midwestern town, closeted with whatever unspeakable misery had caused her to flee?

I felt a kinship for the possibly fled and forlorn girl who, like myself, had no family near her to fall back on, and who possibly shied away from new friends lest she inadvertently give herself away. For whatever deep-seated and mysterious reason that people do odd things, I decided that I had to find her.

On Saturday, I called the Malone number in the phone book. An elderly woman answered with a tentative "Hello?"

"Is this Mrs. Malone?" I asked.

"Yes."

"My name is Emily Menotti. I've lived in Swansea for about ten years now, and I work at the bank. I'm interested in local history, and I came across the story about the disappearance of your daughter, Darcie. I hope I'm not upsetting you by bringing up her name."

"No, dear, it's been a long time. I've made my peace with her loss."

"Could I come by and speak to you about her?"

"I would love to have some company, but could you come tomorrow when my son Albert will be here? He'll remember more about it than I do. I'm eighty-one. I'm starting to forget a lot of things now."

"Okay. How about eleven o'clock in the morning? Would that interfere with church?"

"I don't go anymore, my dear. I can't sit on those hard wood seats. Eleven o'clock will be fine."

When I mentioned to Jack that I was investigating the disappearance of Darcie Malone, he said he had a vague memory of her disappearance. He had been eighteen years old when it happened, the same age as Darcie and Walter. But he'd lived a few miles down the road in Keene and didn't know the families personally.

"The boyfriend probably killed her," he said. "As you and I both know," he continued, "statistics show that you're more likely to be killed by a family member than a stranger. Be careful when you speak to them, although as I recall, they're a tame bunch. But any one of them could have killed her."

"No problem," I told him. "I'll watch what I say. Besides, the mother's eighty-one and Albert's got to be in his fifties. I don't anticipate any violence unless they pull out a gun and try to shoot me."

"Stranger things have happened. You could disappear too."

"Right! If I go missing, have a séance."

"Assuming I want to find you," he teased.

My two friends from high school that I still called once a week were more enthusiastic about my search. "You love a mystery," Janet said. "This is a good one. Keep me posted on what you find."

"Be careful, though," Sue warned me. "If she was killed by someone still living in Swansea, they won't appreciate your digging up the past."

Chapter Two

It was Sunday, September fourteenth when I rang the doorbell at Ten Orchard Road. It took a minute for Mrs. Malone to answer. She slowly opened the weathered wood door with peeling green paint.

She had been a tall woman once, but now she stooped so that her face was level to mine. She had white wisps for hair, fair skin in crinkles all over, and faded blue eyes. She looked older than her eighty-one years. Perhaps the stress of losing Darcie had aged her prematurely. Her smile was kind as she stood back to let me enter. Then she softly closed the door behind us.

Mrs. Malone appeared so thin and frail that it occurred to me that my visit might be too much excitement for her. I followed her as she led me past the dark entrances to the living and dining rooms and motioned me into the kitchen.

The kitchen was a pleasant surprise. Where the outside of the house and the glimpses I caught of the other rooms hinted at dust and neglect, the kitchen was freshly painted a pale yellow and glowed with the late morning sun. There were white lace curtains at the window over the sink, a crisp flowered cloth on the kitchen table, and pink roses in a milk-white vase.

Mrs. Malone wore a lavender knit top with a tan cardigan sweater and loose black slacks. Her feet were swallowed up by plush tan slippers that were matted down with wear but free of dirt or stains. She looked so delicate that I feared for her ability to withstand even a conversation.

"Would you like a cup of tea?" she asked.

"Thank you, yes." I answered, then added, "Your kitchen is lovely, so sunny and bright."

"It's the only room I really live in," she said as she turned on the burner holding the tea kettle.

"I have both my TV," she said, pointing to a small model on the buffet, "and my music." There was a modest stereo tuner and VCR next to the TV. "I don't need anything else."

"I agree. I could be happy here too."

We were quiet for a moment while she fussed with the tea things. She set out matching white mugs, two spoons, sugar, and cream.

"Do you take lemon with your tea?" She asked.

"No. Sugar is fine. Can I help you with anything?"

"I'm fine, dear. Please make yourself comfortable."

While I waited for her, I looked around at the photo collection that adorned the walls. Some were of stern, severely coiffed adults, seeming to glare at the world in disapproval. Then there were happy faces of children opening Christmas presents or posing for the school photographer. Next were vacation shots in front of a government building somewhere and another on a boardwalk by the ocean. The clothes of the people in the pictures were dated, speaking of precious memories going back to the nineteen forties, fifties, and sixties. There were none from the last twenty or thirty years. Time had stopped for the Malone family when Darcie disappeared.

"There you go, dear," Mrs. Malone said as she filled my mug with tea from a china pot. She then poured one for herself and sat down. I wasn't sure where to begin.

"Will Albert be joining us?" I asked, remembering she had mentioned him when I called.

"He'll be along in a minute. He's at the store today doing inventory. He'll just pop in for lunch and to meet you. You said you wanted to ask about Darcie." I admired her bravery at bringing up the subject herself.

I decided to be flat-out honest with her and told her of my experience of standing across the street and hearing the shuffle of footsteps and the man's voice singing Darcie's name.

When I had finished, she looked silently down into her teacup. I honored her silence with my own. After about five seconds, she reached for my right hand. Hers was cool and I could feel her frail bones through the thin flesh. She gripped my right hand with both of hers and said, "Thank God you've heard him too. I thought I was just a crazy old woman."

"Whose voice is it?" I asked.

"My husband's. Darcie's loss destroyed him. He never

recovered, even though he lived for many years afterward. When he became older, ill, and unable to work or sleep well, he used to go out at night and walk the neighborhood, calling her name. And now his spirit can't let go. I hear him myself, sometimes, on a summer evening when the air is damp and heavy. But don't tell Albert. He'll think you're crazy, like me."

"You don't seem crazy to me," I told her.

"Thank you, dear. And now I hear Albert's car in the driveway."

We were quiet again as we listened to a car door slam and heavy footsteps cross the porch. Then we heard the front door open and shut, more heavy footsteps in the hall, and then Albert was in the room, a very tall man with thick brown hair, and a frown on his face. He appeared to be in his late forties or early fifties, without a trace of gray in his hair. He carried the usual middle-age bulge of flesh around his waist. It was his eyes, however, that disturbed me. They were dark brown, not blue like his mother's, and so dark you couldn't tell where the iris ended and pupil began. It was unsettling. I stretched out my hand to introduce myself.

"I'm Emily Menotti, Mr. Malone."

He surprised me by having a warm, soft voice and a strong handshake.

"Glad to meet you. I'm Albert," he said. "I worry about my mother being alone here most of the day. I try to meet anyone who asks to come by to see her."

"I understand. I'd be concerned about my mother too. As I told her on the phone, I'm just doing some research on Swansea and Sussex County history, and I came across Darcie's story in the newspaper."

"Are you doing this as part of an assignment," Albert asked, "or just personal curiosity?" There was an edge to that question, and I chose not to lie. I couldn't blame him. No one wants their personal life exploited for idle curiosity, and that's pretty much what I was doing. But I meant no harm.

"I have to admit it's just a personal interest. I'm not employed by a newspaper or anything like that. I've been researching the local area and came across Darcie's story. Monday through Friday I work as a credit analyst at Sussex County Savings and Loan downtown at Elm and High Streets."

"It's all right, Albert. Really," his mother spoke up. "I'm glad for the company."

"I don't want you upset," he turned and said to her.

"I want to remember Darcie, not forget her," she explained. "It's been so long; sometimes I feel her memory is slipping away. And poor Walter. Everyone assumed he killed her. But I don't think so." She stopped here. Then she rose and chose a photo in an old silver frame and handed it to me.

It showed a family standing in front of this house, and I assumed they were Mr. and Mrs. Malone, Albert, and Darcie. Darcie was tall, thin, and leaning forward just a little, looking sort of gawky and embarrassed. She smiled uncertainly into the camera, as a breeze appeared to blow a wisp of long red hair across her cheek. She was pretty and appealing, like any normal adolescent girl. Albert was a tad taller, with a toothy grin, looking like he was about to play a prank on someone.

"She was a beautiful girl," I said to Mrs. Malone. "What do you think happened the night she disappeared?"

"I don't think about it. I know she's dead. I feel that. But I've given up wondering how it happened. It doesn't change the fact that she's gone."

"What do you think, Albert?" I asked.

Albert seemed not to hear me. He walked to the refrigerator and took out a package of lunch meat and a jar of mustard. I wasn't sure if he was ignoring me, or if he was thinking about his answer. I waited as he took two slices of bread from a loaf on the counter, found a plate for them, and then began to put a sandwich together. He spread the thinnest of films of mustard across the bread and used just one slice of ham for the filling. It seemed such a meager meal. After cutting the sandwich in half and joining us at the table, he finally spoke.

"I've thought about it a lot over the years," he said, in between bites of his lunch. Albert talking with his mouth full was not a pretty sight. "And I've decided, like my mother, that how it happened isn't important. Darcie is gone, Walter has died, and even my father has passed away. What does it matter who killed her?"

"Then you don't think she's still alive?"

"No, I don't. And I don't believe all that Romanov ghost nonsense either."

"Ghost nonsense?" The papers hadn't mentioned ghosts. "What do you mean?"

"You don't know where Darcie and Albert were that night? Where they were having their moonlight picnic?"

"No. I don't remember anything in the newspaper about where the picnic was."

"You didn't grow up around here, did you?" It was almost an accusation, like I had no right to pry into the town's intimate secrets if I weren't a native.

"I moved here ten years ago with my husband. A few years later he left and I stayed. There's something about New Hampshire's dark woods and tall mountains that make me feel at home."

Satisfied with my answer, Albert continued. "They were at the old Romanov mansion, on the other side of town by the river, where Walter was found the next morning. The gossip is that the Romanov mansion is haunted. Even the teenage kids won't hang out there."

"Why do people think it's haunted?"

"In the1920s, Isaac Romanov came here from Europe and opened a bank—the parent of your bank now, only then it was the Swansea Savings Bank. He was in his fifties, a confirmed bachelor, a man obsessed with business and little else, so the story goes. He had devoted his life to amassing a huge fortune. Why he came to Swansea, I never heard. Anyway, he fell in love with one of the young tellers, a beautiful girl named Amanda. They eventually married, and he built her a large home on the Severn River.

"The good news is that Isaac, with Amanda's help, seemed to come out of his shell and join in the Swansea social life. They threw lavish parties, patronized the arts, and gave generously to the local charities. The bad news is that after a few years of a childless marriage, Amanda began an affair with the gardener, and one afternoon Isaac came home from work early and found them in bed together.

"It's an old story," he commented wearily, seemingly dismayed at mankind's unending frailties. "Mature man marries young girl, girl is unfaithful with the household help, and man discovers it and shoots them both. Only this time, Isaac also killed himself after he shot the lovers. He hung himself from the balcony of their upstairs bedroom."

With little emotion or appreciation for the human tragedy that had transpired he continued, "The house was sold a few times, but no one has ever lived there long. That's how the rumors of the haunting began. I have a friend who's a building contractor. He's looked at the property himself. He says there's an underground stream that makes the inside air damp and undermines the foundation. That's the real reason why no one ever lives there for long. Not ghosts. The property has been abandoned since before Darcie and I were born."

"Why would Darcie and Walter have gone there for a picnic?"

"My sister was foolish. She loved ghost stories. She wanted to meet the ghosts personally. And she talked poor Walter into going with her."

Mrs. Malone spoke up, "Darcie thought she was..."

"Mom!" Albert interrupted her. "I don't want you talking about Darcie's silly theories. Not to anyone outside the family. We've had enough bad press as it is. Please."

He turned to me and rose from his seat. "I'm sorry. I think you should leave now. I don't want my mother upset. I have to go back to work, so I'll walk you to your car."

I took the hint and rose from my own seat, gently squeezed Mrs. Malone's fragile hand, and thanked her for her hospitality. Mrs. Malone gazed back at me with intelligent eyes. Her son didn't have to protect her, her eyes told me, but she would let him. She would let him feel like a man.

Albert's manner softened as we walked outside, and he opened my car door for me.

"I'm sorry if I sounded harsh just now, but it's painful for my mother and me to remember Darcie."

I disagreed silently. He was the one upset, not his mother. What I said was, "Of course, but do you mind if I pursue it on my own? I won't contact your mother again. I'll just do some investigating quietly by myself."

"I don't have to be back at the store right away. We're closed today. I'm just checking inventory. I'll be glad to show you the Romanov mansion. We can go in your car if you're comfortable with that."

The change in his attitude was startling, but I had nothing planned for the rest of the day except housekeeping chores, and anything was better than that. "I'd love to go," I said. "Hop in."

Albert was a tall man, but he managed to sit comfortably in the passenger seat of my Honda Civic. "Where to?" I asked as I turned my key in the ignition.

"Head west on Orchard Road until it dead-ends in Cheshire Lane. Then take a right. It's not far."

We didn't speak as we traveled the mile or so past modest wood bungalows to Cheshire Lane. When I turned right, I saw a narrow blacktop road that needed resurfacing and was crowded on both sides with thick trees and bushes. Cheshire Lane led up a small, steep hill. As I crept up it at ten miles an hour, Albert suddenly said, "There, on the left, that driveway."

I turned my car into a driveway that was barely passable due to overgrown bushes that were now dead or diseased. They loomed up eight or ten feet high while their uppermost branches fell sideways creating a canopy over the drive. Their bleakness felt threatening. It was noontime, and yet there was a damp fogginess to the air that gave me goose bumps. After twenty yards or so, we came to a clearing with a circular drive that led to a tall, stucco home painted mustard yellow, with faded white trim and brown shutters. The glass in the windows gleamed dark and forbidding, and I shivered at the thought of coming here at night.

"Your sister came *here* for a romantic picnic?"

"I told you, she was foolish. She wanted to contact the troubled spirits of Amanda and Isaac and help them cross over to the other side. I'm not saying I believe that. It's what she believed."

And what about the spirit of the poor gardener? I thought. *Wouldn't he need help too?*

I parked the car a few feet in front of the entrance. The home was in such disrepair that I didn't trust my car too close to the small roof that extended out over the front door.

"What about Walter? Do you think he believed in ghosts?"

"Walter was just hoping to get laid."

We both climbed out of my car. I didn't dare risk going into the old home, so I walked around the side toward the back. Albert followed me. It was reasonable to assume the police had thoroughly searched the inside of the mansion.

I noticed that the sun had now gone behind the clouds and abandoned us to the gloom of the old building. There were crooked tree limbs covered with naked vines and few leaves. I sensed a general air of fetid decay. As we walked to the back of the house, I noticed that another hundred yards further on and down a steep slope ran the dank green Severn River.

When I reached the back of the house I saw the second-floor balcony, which was accessed from above through French doors, probably the location of the master bedroom. That must have been where Isaac Romanov had hung himself.

"Was there any physical evidence that they had actually been here? And if so, do you know where Walter and Darcie sat when they were here?"

"We found a picnic basket with cheese, crackers, and wine right here near the balcony. We also found their clothes."

"Their clothes? None of the newspaper articles said Walter was naked."

"The *Sentinel* was kind enough to leave that out. They also thought it might be a clue that only the killer would know if, in fact, Darcie was killed."

"And what is your theory?"

"Another man, a spurned boyfriend. Darcie attracted some real weirdos. She could flirt and tease when it suited her, and she usually had one or two low class greasers hanging around."

"You think these guys were capable of violence?"

"Thirty years ago, all the hoods had switchblades and drank heavily. There was a guy named Smitty who used to hang around her and Butch Larson who drove a black Mustang."

"Were they questioned by the police?"

"Of course, but they each had alibis. Claimed to be drinking at a hangout on the other side of town. If Darcie's body had been found, there might have been evidence. But the body was never found."

Albert was somber and thoughtful as we gazed at the old house and the unkempt yard.

"And this tragedy has affected your whole life, hasn't it?" I said softly. "Did you ever marry? Have children?"

"No. Darcie and I were born thirteen months apart. We were very close. I felt as if the better half of me died with her. I still miss her."

Despite the cliché, he seemed sincere. "You don't think she ran off? Was injured, maybe, and forgot who she was? Or was kidnapped and taken somewhere else?"

Albert kicked the dirt and looked around. "No. I don't think so. We would have heard from her by now. Please don't tell anyone what I said about finding the clothes. Swansea has pretty much forgotten about Darcie. My mother and I would prefer she stay forgotten, at least by the general public."

"There's no one for me to tell," I said, dodging the request. "I'm not a journalist. I just wanted to learn what I could about my adoptive hometown."

"Are you remarried or dating someone?"

His question surprised me, but then I wore no rings on my left hand. Jack and I were "friends with benefits." No commitments had been made.

"I date someone occasionally," I told him. "It's not exclusive."

"Would you like to go to dinner and a movie with me sometime?"

His question surprised me. I was also feeling conflicted about Albert. No strong like or dislike at this point, just wariness about his grief-induced bachelorhood and the puritan severity of his thin sandwich. I was more intrigued by his sister's disappearance.

"Yes, I would like that," I told him.

We walked back to the car in companionable silence. He was a gentleman again and opened the driver's side door for me.

On the ride back we spoke of general topics like the amenities of the town and the weather in New England. When I dropped him off at 10 Orchard Road, I gave him my telephone number, and he said he would call. Experience told me there was only a twenty percent chance that he would.

Chapter Three

Monday morning when I returned to work, I questioned some of my coworkers to see if any of them had lived in Swansea thirty years ago, when Darcie disappeared. I discovered that there weren't too many employees aged over thirty, let alone over forty, but there were two women and one gentleman on our customer service team who had grown up here.

The gentleman, Hugh Weaver, was a shade too young. He remembered Butch and the black Mustang. Hugh had admired the upperclassman's car when he first attended Swansea High. He regretted that he was not familiar with Darcie, Albert, Walter Everly, or anyone named Smitty.

The women were old friends who were just a year younger than Darcie and remembered the circumstances of her disappearance. I talked to them as they sat in the cafeteria sipping coffee on their break. They had their own opinions about the Malones, the Everlys, tough-talking greasers with fast cars, and young women who mysteriously vanished while going steady with handsome young men.

"We always thought she went away to have an abortion," said Pat Wainwright.

"And when she didn't return?" I asked.

"We thought she died of complications," said Nina Grant. "Remember, in those days abortion was illegal, and doctors insisted on a parent's permission to even prescribe birth control pills."

"What about Walter winding up in a mental institution?"

"That family was always flaky," laughed Pat. "I'm surprised the whole bunch of them weren't put away."

"Did you like Darcie?'

"She was wild and fun," smiled Nina. "The first to smoke

cigarettes—in fifth grade I think it was. The first to sneak vodka into school dances. It wouldn't have surprised me that she got pregnant before she got married."

This was *not* the Darcie of the newspaper stories, or the sister that Albert had described.

"But her brother was weird," added Pat. "Always seemed a little too bossy of her, I thought, even if he was older. Do you know he went to Yale on a scholarship? And there he is running a hardware store and living with his mother. Something wrong there."

"Do you have any other ideas about Darcie and Walter? What might have happened to them if she didn't die of an abortion? Do you think she and Walter would have married?"

"Of course," said Nina. "They were terribly in love. Everyone could see that."

"And what about Albert? Did he approve of Walter dating his sister?"

"I guess. I never heard different."

"You don't think Albert had anything to do with her disappearance?"

"If he did, it would have been Walter who disappeared," laughed Pat. "He was overprotective of Darcie, maybe even controlling. When Darcie smoked a cigarette, she wasn't rebelling against her parents, she with thumbing her nose at Albert."

"Do you remember someone named Smitty or a guy named Butch who drove a black Mustang?"

"They were both friends of Darcie's. Neither Walter nor Albert liked them," said Pat.

"Would they have attacked Darcie and Walter, maybe hurting Darcie by accident?"

"Hard to say, I didn't know them that well." She added, "I would think, though, that if there had been a struggle there would have been evidence left behind. I'm sure the police investigated that angle."

Good point, I thought. "Do they still live around here?"

"I think they both still live in the area. Smitty, whose real name is Douglas Smith, married Celia Daisy. You remember her, Nina? Curly brown hair and big chest?"

"I do," Nina answered. "And I think Butch, whose last name is Larson, married Laurie Kaiser. They have a garden shop now on Route 202 going south. Both those boys married and had babies right away. Don't know if they're still married to the same girls."

Break time was over and our coffee was gone, so I got up from the table and walked back through the office with them. Returning to my cubicle I thought to myself that if Albert didn't call me, perhaps I would call him.

Chapter Four

It was a warm night in Swansea, New Hampshire, for September. I sat on the wooden front steps of my white shingled rental home and ached for a cigarette. I had quit smoking years ago, but the longing never left me. I needed something to do with my hands, something to keep my physical self placated, and something to keep my body distracted so my mind could relax and think. The tiny rituals of smoking are such a comfort to restless people like me.

I thought about Darcie and her desire to contact the troubled spirits of Isaac and Amanda. I thought about her brother Albert, whose own spirit had never recovered from her disappearance. It seemed odd that his mother had found peace, and not he. It had been my experience, though, that women generally coped with emotional upheaval better than men.

We women buried the dead and moved on, like my own recovery from divorce. Sure, it hurt like hell, and I missed my ex every day those first few years, but life went on. You got up in the morning and went to work, and after six months of denial and then thirty straight days of tears, you went out and met new people. Except for Darcie and Walter and, to a certain extent, Albert. Time had stopped for them. Was Darcie alive somewhere, having experienced some horrendous event on the night of September 6, 1969? Or were her bones hidden in the muddy depths of the Severn River?

A week later, Albert called. He was friendly and polite, asking how I was before mentioning the brilliant leaves on the trees that were beginning to turn red and gold, and then asking if I would like to go to a local restaurant for dinner that Saturday night. Jack and I had no plans. Or rather, Jack might have plans, but he rarely called me before Friday afternoon to discuss them with me. So I accepted Albert's invitation, and we arranged that he would pick me up at 6 p.m. on Saturday.

When I spoke to my friends Janet and Sue later in the week, they both urged caution in my relationship with Albert.

"Carry pepper spray," suggested Janet.

"Make sure you have a hat pin," said Sue.

I appreciated their concern but assured them I would be fine. "If Albert did have anything to do with Darcie's disappearance, he certainly wouldn't want to arouse the suspicions of the police by hurting me."

"Let's hope so," Janet said.

Saturday evening, I was pleasantly surprised when Albert arrived exactly on time. He drove a green 1998 Ford Taurus that was recently washed and vacuumed. Again, he opened the car door for me. I was impressed.

We drove across the river to Saco, and while driving, he asked how my job was and if I'd had a good week at work. I told him my job was pretty boring, but I was glad to have it. The banking industry was in the midst of shipping jobs to India, and I was worried mine would be next.

I asked about the hardware store, and he said things had been slow. New England's was basically a depressed economy. The influx of students to the University of New Hampshire at Keene every September brought in some revenue, but once locks had been changed and microwaves bought, there wasn't much need for a hardware store.

Just past the railroad bridge we turned into the parking lot of the Maine Seafood Company. He suggested I call him Al rather than Albert, and he told me that he knew the owners of the recently opened restaurant.

"Do you like seafood?" he asked.

"Shellfish, not 'fish' fish. I'm sure they'll have lots I like on the menu."

The restaurant was three-quarters full, and we were immediately seated at a booth overlooking the river. Unfortunately, it was already getting dark, so there was little to see on the dock. The electric candles and warm wood paneling created a cozy atmosphere. I was a little at loss for conversation. Along with our jobs, we had discussed the coming fall weather on the trip over, and I didn't have a clue what topic to suggest now.

Albert had asked me what my drink preference was, and when

the waitress appeared I ordered a glass of my favorite white wine, pinot grigio. That, or a good Riesling, is about as close to champagne as I can get without the carbonation and the price tag. Champagne is always my drink of choice, but I know better than to order it on a first date.

Albert ordered a Rusty Nail, a drink I hadn't heard ordered since my twenties. It's a powerful concoction of scotch and Drambuie. I'd long ago given up those types of drinks in favor of headache-free morning-afters.

Once we'd ordered drinks and began perusing the menus, I asked him if he had been born in Swansea, and he surprised me by saying no. He and Darcie had been born in Durbin, Maine, a former shipbuilding community that was now a ghost town since the shipbuilding business had migrated overseas. They had moved to Swansea when he was six, after his father had lost his job at the shipyard. His father would have been content to collect unemployment and welfare in Durbin, but his mother wouldn't hear of it. She insisted there was work in the Swansea area, where she had been born and where her parents still lived.

Albert said his father had been a good student and graduated at the top of his high school class, so his mother's father got Mr. Malone a job at the local high school teaching boat building and other related trades like carpentry and welding. Occasionally, he would substitute for the history and composition teachers. Again, the local newspaper had not been entirely correct.

Our drinks arrived on a tray carried by a tall man with curling black hair wearing a dirty white apron. "Hi, Al," he announced as he neared our table. He looked me over quickly with his sparkling green eyes. "I was tending bar, and when the waitress ordered a Rusty Nail, I knew you were here."

"Hi, Liam," Albert smiled and introduced me. "This is Emily Menotti."

"Liam's the owner," he explained to me. "He used to work for me at the hardware store while he was saving his pennies to open the restaurant. Boy, I miss the days you brought lunch in for the staff."

"Staff?" Liam joked. "And that would be how many? You and me?"

"And whatever kid I had working in the stockroom. How's Peg?"

"My wife," Liam explained as he put our drinks in front of us.

"She's back in the kitchen yelling at the help. That's why I stay in the bar. "

"Enjoy your meal, amigo. And Emily, it was a joy to meet you." Liam turned around and disappeared.

"He looks like fun," I commented.

"More fun than I need sometimes," Albert said. "Now, where were we?"

"You were telling me about when you left Durbin," I answered. "You were very young. Do you remember anything about the town?"

"Only that there were a lot of churches and an equal number of bars. When I was very little we lived with my father's parents. My mother was terribly unhappy living with her in-laws, so we eventually got our own little house. But I think she was just as glad to move away. There's no one there now."

Our salads arrived, and for a while, we were busy with them. I was glad to see he closed his mouth while chewing when dining out. Before we had a chance to start another conversation, my jumbo fried shrimp and Albert's fettuccini with scallops in cream sauce arrived. The meal was excellent. The shrimp was fresh and melted in my mouth. The fries were thin, crisp, and tasty. After the worst of our appetites were sated, he asked how I had come to live in Swansea.

"My husband, who is now my ex," I explained. "He came up here to pursue watercolor painting. I fell in love with New England and decided to stay after the divorce. We never see each other now."

Albert didn't have any comment to that. I've noticed that habit with lots of men. They ask questions and then don't respond to the answers. Who knows why? Must be a male thing. We drifted off into silence again as we finished our meal.

"Would you like dessert?" he asked.

"Would you like to split one?"

"I'd be glad to. Whatever you choose. I like everything."

Albert ordered a slice of cheesecake, which he cut into two. It was creamy and delicious. Sipping coffee, I wracked my brain for something to say.

"Can we talk about Darcie?" I finally ventured.

"I'd rather not. Let's talk about movies. What's your all-time favorite and why?"

"*Close Encounters of the Third Kind,* and it's all about that scene where Richard Dreyfuss is sitting at the dinner table with his family, and he begins building a tower with his mashed potatoes. My second favorite scene is when he starts digging up the plants and dirt from the backyard and throwing them *into* his house through the kitchen window to build a bigger tower in the family room. His wife gets so upset. She can't appreciate that he's had a vision and needs to understand it. I just love his all-out, mad pursuit. The neighbors puzzled looks at his bizarre behavior are so funny. What's your favorite?"

"I guess it would be a football film like *The Whole Nine Yards* or *Friday Night Lights*. I love to watch football."

"Did you ever play?"

"No. I was too tall and skinny and had no coordination. But I attended every game in high school and college."

"Did your college have a good team?" I asked.

"I guess so," was all he said.

Odd for a football fan, I thought.

The bill came and he refused my offer to pay half. I had previously suggested we skip the movies for tonight because I was tired, so Albert drove me home and walked me to my door.

I thanked Albert for the pleasant evening and delicious dinner. He shook my hand, no kiss, and said he would call.

Right, I thought, but smiled anyway. He seemed nice enough if somewhat distant, and I was glad for Jack to have some competition. And Albert was a comforting change from the braggarts and bums I had met at singles' dances. I hoped he would call again after all.

Chapter Five

A month later, on a chilly Saturday morning, I set out for Butch Larson's garden center on Route 202. I headed south and traveled about five miles past the Walmart and an assortment of truck dealerships to the very prosperous Garden World, spread out over two or three acres. It was October, when bush and tree planting are at their height, and the center was abloom with a variety of colorful trees and hardy mums. I parked my car and began to look around.

There weren't a lot of cars in the lot, and not many sales people to answer questions, but after some searching I found an older woman with short, darkly dyed hair. She was Twiggy thin, all bones and angles, which she accentuated with tight black jeans and a thin black jersey. She also wore a head phone with a mouthpiece that she was speaking into. Her eyes were small and cold.

"I'll need 200 more Gold Rush Fever," she was saying to a person or machine on the receiving end when she noticed me. She held up an index finger asking me to wait until she was done. I was glad to wait. She was just a little scary. I think of garden center owners as earth mothers with soft bodies and kind eyes. This woman resembled a shark.

After a few more seconds arranging a delivery time, she signed off to the person or machine and saluted me. "What can I help you with?" she asked.

"Actually, I'm looking for Butch or Laurie Larson. Are either of them here today?"

"You find Butch, you let me know," she said. "I'm Laurie, and the bastard's been gone about a year now. I've no idea where he is. What do you need him for?" She eyed me like I was the competition, maybe an old girlfriend.

"My name is Emily, and I'm doing some private research into

the disappearance of Darcie Malone. Did you know her?"

"Darcie? God, it's been so many years since I thought about her. They never found her body, did they?"

"No. I just saw the old newspaper stories and thought I would ask around. Didn't you go to school with her?"

"Yes and no. We were at the same high school, but we ran in different crowds. She was flighty and artistic. My gang was into hot cars and booze. Get the picture?"

"Did Butch ever date her?"

"Butch didn't date. Butch took you for a ride in his precious black Mustang, got you drunk, and then had his way with you. That's what our crowd did. When the girls got pregnant, we married. You had your fun then you paid your dues."

Sounded like a wonderful life.

"So, he wasn't friends with Darcie?"

"I'd say they were acquaintances. Butch had the hots for her. Darcie was naïve. She didn't understand that she shouldn't act friendly with him out of politeness. She would smile at him and say "hello," and "how are you," and Butch would take that as encouragement. He asked her more than once to go for a ride in his Mustang. She always turned him down. Then he'd call her a tease. But she wasn't a tease, just stupid."

"Do you think he spoke to her or saw her on the night she disappeared?"

Laurie paused for a second here and looked up at the sky as if searching for an answer up there. After a bit, she returned her gaze to me.

"No. We were all drinking that night—'we' being Butch, me, Smitty, and Celia. We were on the other side of town at a bar that served minors, nowhere near the Romanov place. Never saw her or Walter. Never heard anything, either. That's what we told the police and that's the truth."

I thought it odd she needed to convince me. "What was the name of the bar? Is it still there?"

"It's there, half a block from the riverfront on Third Street. It's a name you don't forget, the Crucifixion Bar and Grill. And I'll bet they still serve minors."

"You have any theories about what happened to Darcie?"

"I always thought Walter was a little strange. And his turning up the next morning without her pretty much says it all. I figured he raped her, killed her, and threw her in the river. Everyone thought that. As I recall, though, there was never any evidence to prove it."

"Did Butch have a different theory?"

"Butch doesn't have theories. All he has are binges and hangovers. You find him, you tell him I'm looking for him. He owes me for medical bills. I've got to get back to work now."

"Thanks for your help, Laurie. Do you know where I could find Smitty and his wife?"

"The Universal Life Church in downtown Swansea. Smitty's a minister now. I don't see them much anymore."

"Thanks again," I said and wondered just how much of what Laurie had just told me was true.

Chapter Six

Since it was still early afternoon, I headed back into town and looked for the Universal Life Church. Laurie had said downtown, and downtown Swansea is about five blocks long and two blocks wide, with the east side sloping down to the river. At Fifth and High Streets was the church, if you could call it a church. The building looked like an old movie theater, with cheap cardboard signs in red, blue, and yellow lettering, announcing times for services and Sunday school. The doors were locked, but one sign had a number to call for more information and the name of the Reverend Douglas Smith. I jotted the number down on an old receipt I had in my purse.

Since I was already in town, I decided to go looking for the bar where Butch, Smitty, and their girlfriends had claimed to be on the night of Darcie's disappearance. Laurie had said Third Street, just two blocks away.

The sky darkened at that moment, and the wind suddenly blew bitter cold as I followed the brick sidewalk down High to Third. I shivered with the unexpected chill. As I turned toward the river at Third Street, a gust of wind nearly blew me backwards. I shivered again and kept going, head down and arms wrapped tightly across my chest. The clouds that were blotting out the sun now let loose with stinging pellets of rain.

Halfway down the block I saw a red neon sign in a small window across the street. The neon tubing formed a red crucifix followed by the words "Bar and Grill." I stepped off the curb to cross over and suddenly smacked into something large and metal, knocking me backwards and onto my derriere. I sat in the street, stunned and shaking. What had just happened?

There was a simultaneous screech of car brakes and then a man's voice. "What're you doing, lady? You walked right into the side of my car!"

I looked up. Damn if the man didn't look like an aging Jesus, with shoulder length brown hair and a long, graying beard. He had large, liquid brown eyes and a pale complexion. I was still in shock and couldn't find my voice.

"Are you alright?" he asked.

I thought about it for three or four seconds. I didn't feel any pain, except in my rear end. I looked at my arms and legs—no blood. "I guess I'm okay."

"Can I help you up?"

"Yes," I gratefully accepted. "I was going over to that bar. Could you walk me over?"

"I think you've had enough to drink, ma'am," he said as he took my elbow and helped me stand.

"No, I haven't been drinking. I was just distracted. I'm sorry. I guess I walked into your car."

His look said he didn't believe me. He took a card from his wallet and handed it to me. It read "The Reverend Douglas Smith, Universal Life Church."

"I was just looking for you, up at your church," I told him excitedly. "I'm Emily Menotti. Laurie Larson told me how to find you. Can we talk? Can I buy you a cup of coffee or a drink?"

"I'm in recovery fifteen years now, and I don't think you should be drinking either. Let's try that Starbucks® at the bottom of the hill. I'll park my car and meet you there."

The sun came out again just then, and I noticed the wind had died down. "See you there," I agreed.

I continued slowly down Third—mentally checking my limbs for damage—down to where the street met the Severn River at a boulevard appropriately titled "The Riverfront." Starbucks® was on the corner. Is there a town in America that doesn't have a Starbucks®? It was nearly deserted at this time of the afternoon.

I waited for the reverend before ordering coffee, and when he arrived we both got mocha lattes and found a small round table. I was still a bit shaken up by my encounter with the reverend's gray Camry, but I didn't seem to be hurt anywhere. There was some dirt on my coat sleeves where I had made contact with the side of the car, but that was the extent of the damage.

"So why were you looking for me?" he asked.

"I'm investigating the disappearance of Darcie Malone. I know you knew her in high school. I just wondered if you had any thoughts or theories about what happened."

"Are you a reporter?"

"No, I'm embarrassed to say I'm just a nosy newcomer—newcomer, that is, ten years ago. I wasn't here when she disappeared."

"Have you read the newspaper articles?"

"Yes, but I'm finding they aren't always correct. They said Darcie was shy and bookish. Her classmates seem to disagree."

"Well, you know some people are shy when you first meet them, but they can have a wild side that they save for when they get comfortable with you."

"And Darcie was like that?"

"I'd say so. She was quiet in school, and she got good grades, but she and her friends used to have slumber parties where they all smoked cigarettes and drank Southern Comfort. In the 1960s that's about as rowdy as most girls in Swansea knew how to get. Marijuana hadn't found its way to our little town yet."

"Who were her friends? Did you know her well?"

"Her friends mostly left town after high school. Penny somebody-or-other got married and moved to DC with her lawyer husband. There was a friend named Patty who married an airline pilot, and she moved away. I think there was another Patty who went to one of those Jesuit universities and never came back either. Darcie did well in school, but she never wanted to go to college. She disappeared that September after we graduated from high school. I don't remember if she was working at a job or not."

"I understand you and your friends were at the Crucifixion Bar and Grill up the street here that night she disappeared."

"Well, we were for a while. As I recall, we got drunk and then went skinny-dipping in the river, but we were a good half mile from the Romanov place."

"You never heard any screams or calls for help, or saw Walter wandering around?"

"No, ma'am. We were making quite a bit of noise ourselves, I do believe. The cops spoke to us the next day, but we couldn't help them."

"What do you think happened?"

"What everyone else thinks. Walter killed her. Probably threw her body in the river."

"And his madness? Was that an act?"

"Walter wasn't the killer type. I don't think he ever even had a fist fight like most boys do when they're growing up. I think she probably did something like refuse to have sex, and he got angry and forced himself on her and maybe accidentally killed her. Then he couldn't live with what he'd done."

"You make it sound so cut and dry, like men have the right to demand sex."

That seemed to offend him, and on second thought, I decided that I hadn't chosen my words too wisely. I really wasn't accusing Walter of rape; maybe just taking advantage of a young girl's naïveté.

The reverend looked at me silently for five seconds or so. In that time, I noticed how the brown of his hair didn't match the brown sections of his graying beard. The good reverend dyed his hair.

"We're not a sophisticated group here in Swansea," he began. "I admit I ran with a rough crowd back then, but even the good boys and girls had sex at the drive-in on Saturday night. I bought booze more than once for Darcie when her girlfriends had a sleepover. That was pretty much what our relationship was. I hung around her trying to get her to go out with me, and she teased me just enough to let me buy her beer and Southern Comfort, but she wouldn't get in my car. She wouldn't even get into Butch's Mustang, and lots of girls would have put out for a chance to ride around in that car."

"Not so different, really, than where I grew up. Are you still married to Celia?"

"Proud to say I am, and we've got three beautiful daughters and one grandson."

"Does Celia agree with you about Darcie?"

"No. She says Albert did it."

"Why?"

"She just didn't like him, that's all. No good reason. I've got to go now. Celia is expecting me. You keep that card and give me a call if I can ever be of any help to you. You might even try coming to church some Sunday. We respect all denominations. We have something for everybody."

"Thank you, Reverend."

"Call me Doug. And watch where you're walking."

"Will do."

I sat at the table a while longer, gazing through the windows at the peeling white paint of the boats tied up to the docks. The Severn was not a wide river and had little industry other than recreational boating, fishing, and a dockside restaurant or two. I wondered if buried in its mud and sludge lay the pale bones of one teenage girl named Darcie Malone.

The sky had turned gray again, and evening was coming on with a damp chill. I decided to forget the Crucifixion bar for the day and head back to my cozy home and a good mystery story.

When I spoke to Janet and Sue on Tuesday evening of the following week, Sue said, "I'm writing all this information down, just in case something should happen to you."

"I'll be fine," I assured her. "No one ever takes me seriously."

Chapter Seven

I'm not much of a bar person, and the idea of going back into town and visiting the Crucifixion Bar and Grill lost its appeal after a while. I'd been incredibly lucky with complete strangers being willing to talk to me about Darcie, but I was hesitant to try my luck by myself in what might be a pretty rough environment. I felt temporarily stalled in my research.

Snow came in November and turned Swansea into a cobalt-blue-skied, white-frosted fairyland. Some of the older homes had bright red metal roofs that heated up in the sunshine and encouraged the snow to melt and not weigh too heavy on the roof. I didn't even mind shoveling the first flakes off my little bit of sidewalk that led from the front door to the street. Southeastern New Hampshire had few steep hills, so I drove easily to work and the grocery store in my Civic.

Albert called and suggested we go to the movies one Saturday night. I hadn't heard from Jack for a few weeks and was considering myself unofficially dumped, so I agreed.

He remembered that I liked science fiction, so he suggested the old *The War of the Worlds* movie that was showing at a science fiction festival at a local theater. I had read the book and knew the story of the '30s' broadcast that had panicked folks in New Jersey. He also suggested we go to the early show and then to a diner afterwards for something to eat.

I loved the movie and found Albert a comfortable companion. He had seen all my favorite sci-fi movies of the fifties; he'd watched *The Twilight Zone* with Rod Serling and *Thriller* with Boris Karloff on TV. Best of all, his favorite show of the '90s was also mine, the *X-Files*. In a tall, thin, brown-eyed way Albert could even remind me a little of David Duchovny.

After the movie, over hamburgers and sundaes, we discussed our favorite episodes, his being the spooky Halloween show with the two-headed boy in love with Cher, and mine being the one where Peter Boyle foretells Mulder's death from autoerotic asphyxiation. I never got around to pumping him for more information on Darcie.

When Albert finally drove me home, I was actually hoping he would kiss me, but he didn't. Nor did he promise to call.

Chapter Eight

Thanksgiving came and went and Albert began calling once or twice a week in the evening to chat. He told me about business at the hardware store and how slow it was this time of year. He, in turn, listened to my stories of office intrigue and home repair adventures.

We went out for breakfast a few times, and then dinner again at the Maine Seafood Company. But there were still no signs of physical affection, and I was never invited to the house. I wasn't hungry for physical contact, but I did wonder why he had no interest. Like any woman, I enjoy reassurances that I'm still attractive. Maybe he was just keeping an eye on me to see where my interest in his sister would go. Unfortunately, I had been too busy to pursue it any further.

Early in December I attended a holiday cocktail party given by my boss. He had a large old home that had been remodeled with rows of tall windows that shone with electric candles, now aglow, in the dusk of the December evening. Red ornaments on a huge fir tree in the front parlor window gleamed with warmth and festivity. I found myself a glass of pinot grigio and made small talk with the women in customer service and the guys in IT.

While spearing a square of cheddar cheese with a toothpick at the hors d'oeuvres table, I bumped elbows with a gentleman in a gray tweed blazer, nearly knocking his drink out of his hand. I started to apologize for my clumsiness when he turned to face me, and I was stopped midsentence by the most gorgeous blue eyes I'd even seen. They weren't Paul Newman china blue, but soft and smoky with hints of gray like star sapphires. They took my breath away. All at once I lost my voice.

"No, excuse *me*," he said. "I wasn't looking. Are you okay?"

I was not okay. I was overwhelmed with desire for this man, for this stranger, who might have been a criminal or a serial killer or god knows what. He looked at me with concern. He probably thought I was the dumbest old lady he'd ever met in his entire life, which life span looked to be roughly the same as mine.

After a few seconds I recovered, put down my glass, and held out my hand.

"Emily Menotti," I said. "And you?"

"Bill Moore," he said. "And what's a nice girl like you doing in a place like this?"

The cliché was spoken lightly, with a mocking half-smile from the pale-haired man who was standing there tall and handsome like the answer to a single woman's prayer.

"Our host, Roger, is my manager at the bank," I said, totally flubbing my opportunity for a witty rejoinder that would impress the hell out of him. I added, "I'm a credit analyst. Yourself?"

"Reporter." He said. "Not that I'm here officially. I'm just a friend of Roger's."

"Reporter, as in the *Sussex Sentinel*?"

"Yes. I'm the Swansea bureau. The main office is in Concord."

Hello, Darcie, I'm back on case!

"Did you grow up here?" I asked.

"Right here in Swansea. My parents had a restaurant in town. They've passed now and my brother runs it. Have you been to the Chart Room?"

"The restaurant that's a restored yacht in the harbor? No, I haven't, but I've heard it's wonderful. You weren't interested in pursuing the family business?"

"I was never into it. I'm too restless. Always looking for a good story."

"The most interesting story I've heard in the ten years I've been here is the story of Darcie Malone, the girl who disappeared in September 1969. Do you remember anything about it?"

"My mother's maiden name was Everly. Walter's father was her brother."

Insert foot, turn red, wish you were dead.

"I'm so sorry! I can't seem to stop causing you pain. Please forgive me. Can we talk about movies or TV, or maybe movies on TV?"

"Let's sit down," he said kindly, and motioned to an empty

section of a nearby sofa. It was parallel to a small wood fire in a large fieldstone fireplace. I was only too glad to sit down. I would have liked even better to sink into the cushions and be swallowed up, away from this tête-à-tête that was turning into a disaster. I did notice, however, that there was no ring on the telling finger of his left hand.

"I can talk about it; I don't mind," he said graciously. "Did you have a specific question?"

I was embarrassed now to have intruded on a family tragedy. "Not really," I lied. "It's the mystery of it all that intrigues me. I've been to the Romanov house. It's a little spooky."

"Did you go by yourself?"

"No," I said and knew that now I was really in trouble. What would he think of my going to the house with Albert? Ah, well, he might be married after all and just not wearing a ring.

"Albert took me there."

His drink stopped midair. "Albert?"

"Do you think he had anything to do with Darcie's disappearance?"

"No, I don't think he had anything to do with his sister's disappearance. Are you and he dating?"

I decided to sidestep that one. "I was visiting his mother, who I thought was just a wonderful woman, and we were talking about Darcie, and he offered to take me to the old mansion where it all happened. That was way back in September. We've gone out a few times, but it's very casual." Part of me chided me for babbling like a crazed teenager, but I was too emotional to care.

Bill looked at me with that question in his eyes of whether or not he was talking to a sane person.

"He wouldn't talk about Darcie, either," I added.

"So, I gather your interest in him has more to do with the mystery surrounding Darcie than any romantic attachment?"

"Sort of—and your poor family, to lose a cousin under such circumstances. I'm so sorry. Were you and Walter close?"

"No, not at all. Our families only got together on the major holidays even though we lived right here in town. My mother used to refer to her brother as a beatnik—remember beatniks? Remember Maynard G. Krebs? He was always my favorite character on TV when I was growing up."

"Too bad your father had a restaurant and not a coffee house.

I had an older brother who flirted with it a bit. He loved poetry and folk music. He introduced me to Peter, Paul and Mary, and the Kingston Trio."

"Do you still have any albums?"

"No, they all got warped over time and many moves. You?"

"No. My ex-wife took them all with her when we divorced. That was one of the things that we enjoyed in common. You're not married, right? I mean, the dates with Albert and all."

"Divorced too. It's been five years. I'm comfortable with it now."

"Me too. It's been seven years for me. Kids?"

"No, I could never talk my ex into it. You?"

"Me neither. Well then, I think I should take you to the family restaurant some evening and introduce you to fine dining. Would you be interested?"

"I would love to go." I pulled out a business card and wrote my home phone number on it.

"Call me when you get hungry," I said.

He smiled at the double meaning and handed me a card of his own with the home number already included.

We spent the rest of the evening talking about where all the old folk singers were now, and then I left around nine. As I trod carefully down the sidewalk through the cold wind and drifting snow I felt warm and cozy within, thinking of how attractive and companionable Bill Moore had been. And, as a bonus, he was related to the Darcie Malone mystery. "Darcie," I whispered to the night air, "I'm coming to get you."

CHAPTER NINE

Bill called the day after Christmas and asked me out to dinner for New Year's Eve. As I had no plans except to watch TV, I gladly accepted. Albert hadn't called for a week, so I was guessing he wouldn't be asking me out for that holiday. On the morning of December twenty-seventh, I floated back to work, after a quiet Christmas with my dreams and my music, and wondered how I would be able to concentrate on my work for the next few days. That thought turned out to be the least of my problems.

It's funny how just the air in a building can transmit emotion. I could sense it the moment I walked off the elevator and onto the floor. There was just this sense that something major had transpired, and that doom and gloom were lurking in the corners.

My manager, Roger, usually smiling and relaxed, appeared at my desk and said only, "Conference Room Two, five minutes." Then he walked away.

Conference Room Two was the largest conference room on our floor, so I guessed this was not a one-on-one meeting. The other credit analyst I worked with, a stunning African-American woman named Keisha Deputy, was already pushing in her chair and grabbing a notepad and pen. I did likewise and we headed for the conference room together.

"Do you know what's up?" I asked her.

She shook her head "no."

There was grim silence in the conference room. Then two customer service supervisors trickled in with coffee cups and serious faces. Meaningful glances were exchanged. No one expected good news.

Roger finally entered, and with him was the site manager for Sussex County Savings and Loan.

Roger began, "Good morning, and thank you for being here. I hope you all had an enjoyable holiday with your families." He paused so we could all nod "yes."

"You know Pete, our site manager. We're going to participate in a conference call with Win Bryson, the president of Sussex County Savings and Loan. Pete's going to dial in now."

With that, Pete—a medium tall, brown-haired, middle-aged gentleman who was painfully thin and worked to disguise a faint tremor in his right hand—reached across the large polished wood table to where the conference call phone sat. He dialed a number, punched in a code, and then Win could be heard on the speaker, loud and serious, welcoming us to the call and hoping we had all had a pleasant holiday with our families.

"The purpose of this call," he finally said, "is to announce the sale of Sussex County Savings and Loan to Metrobank." He paused. We stopped breathing. "To be finalized by the end of the first quarter, March 31st, 2000." We all started to breathe again. Three months. We had three months to find new jobs.

"I know this is upsetting news," he continued. "But our merger with Metro will actually benefit our stockholders and create an opportunity for growth for all of us." Win, the spinmeister. I could see how excited everyone was—not. I saw panic in more than one pair of eyes. Roger and Pete looked serious rather than shocked. They had obviously known this was coming.

"Pete and Roger will speak to you about the details for your site. We're not closing any offices down just yet. We'll be consolidating certain responsibilities so that functions are not unnecessarily duplicated among our departments. Roger and Pete will continue to report to me, but my title will change from President of Sussex County Savings and Loan to President of the Southeastern New Hampshire Affiliates for Metrobank. My new job will include not just the site in Swansea, but also the Metrobank sites in Concord and Durham." Old Win had turned the whole thing into a promotion for himself and probably for his cronies as well. And where would the rest of us end up?

"Are there any questions?"

You didn't get to the Exempt status, as all of us in the room were, by arguing, crying, or making negative comments about upper management decisions, especially to the big guy, so we sat there in stunned silence and waited for the dust to settle.

"Thank you for your time," Win continued after a short pause. "I'll turn you over now to Roger and Pete. Good-bye."

The speaker went dead, and Roger and Pete looked quickly at each other, communicating courage, like buddy corporate soldiers bravely facing the enemy. I kept to my usual mode of corporate survival — eyes down and mouth shut.

"What happens to customer service?" Joan D'Angelo, a customer service supervisor, spoke first.

Roger answered, "There are no plans at the moment to move our customer service functions. It will actually be beneficial for Metrobank to have more than one site in case of severe weather or power outages. Your reps will have to learn a few more products so that they can handle calls from Metrobank customers, but we'll provide training over the next three months."

"And Credit?" asked Keisha.

Pete looked at us and replied calmly, "The credit function will move to the Metrobank offices in Boston. Roger and I will meet with each of you individually later this morning and discuss possible options for continued employment."

I was losing my job, pure and simple — me, a single woman, fifty-plus years of age, the most unwanted commodity on the face of the earth. I thought of my salary, which at $48,000 wasn't terrific, but it was a whole lot more than the starting salary somewhere else; and of my four wonderful weeks of vacation that I would lose; and of the retirement benefits I had accrued after ten years of service and had hoped to stretch into twenty. There was no way to recoup at another institution what I was about to lose at the hands of Metrobank.

Pete continued, "I will arrange meetings with the customer service teams this morning. Joan, why don't you tell your group to log off and come in here first? Then we'll talk to Don's group," he nodded at Don Wilson, the other customer service supervisor. "And then I'll speak to Keisha and Emily. I'd appreciate it if you wouldn't speak about this to anyone else this morning until I've had a chance to meet with everyone. Thank you for your time." We were dismissed.

Keisha and I returned to our desks. We were not in a mood to work, so we decided to go downstairs to the cafeteria and get coffee. Then we sat at a table and listened for a moment to the soft murmuring going on at other tables in the room.

"What do you think?" I asked Keisha, who at age twenty-five, with a brand-new MBA in Business Administration, would probably have a job by the end of January.

"I think I'm going to get the hell out of banking. For the past five years all we've seen is consolidation upon consolidation. Chase merged with Chemical then with Bank of New York and then with JPMorgan. Bank One used to be First USA; Maryland National Bank merged with Bank of America. Citibank bought Associates National Bank and Travelers, and god knows who else. In a few years Metro will merge with one of them and who knows what will happen. I'm outta here. What about you?"

"I don't know what I'll do. I actually love my job. The only other job I've ever had that I liked as much was when I was a bookkeeper for a day care center, but the pay was terrible. Day care is probably the only industry that pays less than banking."

"Do you think they'll offer you a job in Boston?"

"You mean allow me to apply for one if they happen to be hiring?"

"Of course—silly me," Keisha laughed.

"They'd have to double my salary to live in the Boston area, and I'm sure they won't. I don't want to leave Swansea. I've been here ten years, I love my little house. The big city doesn't appeal to me at all."

"Then I'll see you at the unemployment office."

"Right! With your good looks and credentials I doubt you'll skip a paycheck."

"We'll see. But seriously, Emily, what do you think Pete is going to say to you?"

"Good-bye and good luck. That's all I expect."

With that, we finished our coffee and wandered silently back to our desks. Then we spent the rest of the morning surfing Monster.com and other employment websites to assess our "opportunities for growth." They looked pretty grim to me.

Right before lunch, Roger called me.

"Can you come to my office for a moment?"

"Of course, I'll be right there." This was it. My stomach churned. My mouth felt dry. I grabbed a cinnamon Tic Tac hoping for relief.

Pete was not there, only Roger, looking calm and prepared. I sat down opposite him and said nothing, inwardly steeling myself for the worst.

"You've been with us for ten years, Emily. As you know, we're moving the credit functions to Boston. However, we're keeping our customer service department and expanding their responsibilities."

I nodded, not sure where this was going.

"I understand you have some training background."

Again, I nodded. Before moving to New Hampshire I had been a credit trainer for Chase in Wilmington, Delaware.

"We'd like to offer you a position as a trainer for the customer service team. You'll need extensive training yourself, but we can provide that. Are you interested?"

Was I interested? I could have hugged him.

"I'd love to" was what I said.

"I'll get back to you with the details, but I guess I should warn you, we're letting Keisha go. I hope it's not awkward for you."

Yes, it was going to be awkward, but I could handle it.

As way of dismissal, he held out his hand to shake. I shook it and then walked slowly back to my desk, passing Keisha on the way, headed for her own meeting.

Later that afternoon, as I struggled to focus on my work, Keisha stopped by my desk and asked me to come to the cafeteria with her. It was closed this time of day, so we had the place to ourselves. I wondered what she was going to say. Would she be angry at me for being offered a new job?

"They're letting me go," she said.

"I'm sorry," was all I could think of.

"You've been here longer than me, Emily," she added. "I understand why they're keeping you."

"They offered me a training job with customer service." There was no point in lying.

"Congratulations. I think you'll do a wonderful job."

"I'm sorry, Keisha. I'll miss you. I wish there was something I could do."

"I'll let you know," she said.

That evening, Albert called. He didn't ask about New Year's Eve, but he did ask how work was. I told him I was losing my job at the end of January but that I might have a position in a different area of the bank. I tried to sound nonchalant, like I lost jobs all the time.

"I can always use someone with credit background in the office at the hardware store," he said. "All the payables and receivables get to be too much for me in the spring and fall when we're busiest. If you can't find anything, I'd be glad to hire you. I can't offer you the kind of money you're probably making now, but I could offer ten dollars an hour."

It was very sweet of him. I'm sure he didn't have much profit to work with.

"Thank you, Al, but I'm hopeful the job I was offered with the new owners will work out."

"I'll keep it open for you."

"Okay."

Well, if I took his job offer, we would certainly have lots of opportunity to talk about Darcie.

Word gets around quickly in small towns, especially when a plant is closing or a shop is shutting its doors. Everyone who banked at Sussex County Savings and Loan, which would be at least half the town—the other competitor being the local credit union (where I would be sending my resume)—knew their bank had been gobbled up by the big guy. I didn't totally trust the bank to follow through on the new job.

Standing in line at the dry cleaner's a day later, who should walk in the door but the Reverend Douglas Smith. He recognized me immediately and surprised me by knowing about the bank merger.

"Will you lose your job?" he asked after saying "Hello."

"I might have a position with the new bank," I told him.

"We need a church secretary," he said. "The pay is terrible, but you can get free breakfast and lunch with the day care center staff in their cafeteria. If you're interested, the job is yours."

"You don't even know if I can type!"

"Trust me, in a small town I know more about you than you think."

That almost sounded like a threat, but he was offering a job.

"That's very kind of you, but I'm hoping to stay in banking. If that doesn't work out, Albert has offered me a job at the hardware store."

"You trust him?"

That spooked me too. What else did the good reverend know? I was getting my dry cleaning and getting out of there.

"Thank you" was all I said, then I paid for my clothes and left.

When I spoke to Janet and Sue that evening, they were both sympathetic and encouraging.

"You loved training," Janet reminded me. "You'll do fine."

"And if it doesn't work out, you can always move back to Wilmington again and get a job here," Sue suggested when I spoke to her.

"But I love living here," I explained. "And I can't leave until I find out what happened to Darcie."

Chapter Ten

New Year's Eve was cloudless and frigid. I wore a black knit dress with long sleeves and a plunging V neckline. I was sure this was going to be a wonderful evening. There would be good food, intelligent company, and hopefully a lot more information about Darcie Malone.

The only worry on the horizon was the Y2K issue. Every business, utility, and government office was concerned about the computer industry's ability to deal with a year ending in "00." There were wild scenarios of nationwide computer failures plunging the continent into darkness and financial records disappearing into an abyss of techno hell. I wasn't worried. I'd be up to any challenge with my hot date at my side.

Speaking of which, Bill picked me up at eight-thirty, looking more handsome than I remembered. The soft dark wool of his overcoat brought out the smoke in his blue eyes. To match the brilliant stars above, he wore a few glistening snowflakes in his hair.

He escorted me to his black Lexus four-wheel drive, and we headed into downtown Swansea. On our way to the riverfront, we drove down Third Street right past the Crucifixion Bar and Grill. The red neon sign glowed blood red amid the black of the night and the white dust of snow. I pointed it out to Bill.

"Ever been there?" I asked.

"Sure, in high school. Now it's where all the crazy Vietnam vets hang out. I'd avoid it if I were you."

"Did you get drafted? Did you serve in Vietnam?"

"I was old enough to have graduated from college when the lottery began. I had a low number. When I finally got drafted, I lucked out with a cushy job in Germany for three years. The vets hate me."

"No wonder you don't go in there."

He didn't respond to that. We had arrived at the Chart Room, and Bill was out of the car immediately. He helped me out and we walked up the spacious, carpet-covered plank to board the boat that had become a restaurant. It glowed with wraparound glass windows and electric lights. There were pine branches and sparkling ornaments for Christmas. The carpet and chair cushions were red. We were shown to a white linen-covered table by a window. White candles flickered on brass stands. Pine boughs and red carnations created a festive centerpiece.

Bill helped with my chair and asked what I wanted to drink. "Grey Goose® martini on the rocks," I said, "with a twist." A young man appeared and introduced himself. "Good evening, Mr. Moore. I'm Dan and I'll be your server this evening. Would you like to start with drinks?"

Bill gave him our order, which was two Grey Goose® martinis on the rocks. The server handed us tall menus and explained that the specials were rock lobster tail stuffed with crabmeat or filet mignon in wine sauce. Then he excused himself to get our drinks.

I loved the menu. Dining out is dicey for me as I have the palette of a bad-tempered two-year-old. The Chart Room, however, accommodated multiple tastes with selections from meat, fish, fowl, and creative vegetarian dishes. I pondered the lobster tail, which I love, but knew it was probably the most expensive item on the menu. Not a good move on a first date.

"I'm getting the filet," Bill said. "Feel free to order that or the lobster tail. I get a discount being a relative."

Could this evening get any better? "I would love to have the lobster tail. Does it come with salad or side dishes?"

"Both, or soup if you prefer. I usually get the salad and the house veggies. I also recommend the rolls. My sister-in-law created the recipe."

Our drinks arrived and I was suddenly at a loss for words. Bill seemed content to relax in silence and sip his drink. I finally asked him, "How long have you been a reporter?"

"Since I left the army. I did a little radio news in Germany for the troops, and I liked getting all the AP and UPI reports. It made me feel like I knew what was happening before everyone else did. When I got back to the states, I broke the bad news to my father that I wasn't interested in the restaurant business and got a job on the

Sussex Sentinel. I've been there ever since. And you...you said you worked at the bank?"

"I'm in transition. I was a credit analyst. I used to read credit reports and make recommendations for personal loans. But Sussex County Savings and Loan was bought by Metrobank, which I'm sure you've heard of, and that function is being moved elsewhere, so I'm going to be a customer service trainer when my own training is finished. I'm not thrilled about it—I loved my old job—but it's better than being let go."

"The country seems to be bank merger crazy right now. I guess it's the global economy. They're sending as many jobs as possible to India because the labor is cheap, and then the employees who do keep their jobs here are so grateful that they gladly work fifty or sixty hours a week. It's a win-win for corporate. You've got it tough."

Salads arrived and we fell silent except for muffled sounds of eating. But, first, I had to remove all the tomatoes, cucumbers, peppers, and mushrooms from my salad. That left some greens, some onion, and lots of blue cheese dressing. Bill was a gentleman and didn't comment on my eccentricity.

We chatted about the Y2K scare that tonight all the computer systems in the country would fail to negotiate the change from 1999 to 2000—both of us thought there would be no problem—and then moved on to general topics like TV and movies as we finished our salads. When the main courses arrived—my lobster tail was huge and delicious—we moved on to books we had both read and favorite authors. Bill was a fan of science fiction and chess strategies.

About halfway through dinner, an older man and woman approached our table. The man resembled Bill, only a bit grayer, and the woman was plump with attractively styled brown hair.

"My brother, John, and his lovely wife, Bernice," Bill said when they stopped. He started to rise from the table.

"No, no, please don't get up," said John. "We don't want to spoil your meal, only to meet your lovely date. Emily, am I right?"

He had a charming, mannered voice, and I smiled in acknowledgement.

"This is a wonderful restaurant," I told him. "The meal is superb, not to mention how delicious the rolls are."

Bernice smiled and glowed. "I'm so glad you like them," she responded in a thick southern drawl.

"As you can tell," John added, "They are a southern recipe."

"The best in the U S of A," I offered.

"Well, we won't disturb you any longer. Please let us know if there is anything you need," John said as they turned to leave.

"I'll call you tomorrow," Bill said as they were leaving. Then to me, "Hope you didn't mind their coming by to see you."

"Not at all. I would have been disappointed if they didn't." And I meant it.

Bill mentioned that there was a New Year's Eve party at a friend's house. Did I want to go? Of course! I begged off dessert thinking there might be some interesting snacks at the party, and we both finished the meal with coffee, Bill's regular and mine hazelnut. New England inns and restaurants serve the most fragrantly soothing coffees in the world, and hazelnut is my personal favorite.

We left without paying, and Bill explained where we were going next, across the Severn River to a spanking new home where there would be live music and lots of champagne. His friend, Rialto Diaz, owned a chain of beauty salons in New Hampshire and southern Maine, and he and his wife had just moved in the day before Christmas. This was a combination housewarming and New Year's celebration for all their friends.

"Did Rialto grow up here also?" I asked.

"Yes, he did. His great-great-grandfather was the infamous gardener at the Romanov home. But don't bring it up. He doesn't like to talk about it. Thinks it's unlucky. He tends to be passionate and quick-tempered. His wife, Stella, is the opposite. She's a dyed-in-the-wool Stepford wife from the Hamptons on Long Island. You'll never get a real opinion or a real feeling out of her, and I've been trying for twenty years."

"What a couple! But I have to applaud twenty years of marriage."

We turned off the road and passed between two tall stone pillars with black iron gates pulled open. Two short turns in the drive and you broke through the shrubbery to view a pale stucco mansion with a porte cochere and a paved brick turnaround. Lights blazed from curtainless windows, and decorative wrought iron balconies graced the upper story. The thump of bass instruments vibrated through the cold night air.

We were met at the door by a tall, handsome man who gave the impression of a wealthy gypsy—lots of wild dark hair and huge excited eyes.

"I am Rialto," he greeted me. He nodded to Bill then turned his attention back to me. "And you must be the beautiful Emily I've heard so much about."

"You're too kind. Thank you so much for inviting me to your home. It's gorgeous."

"Thank you, lovely lady. May I help you with your coat?"

After disposing of our coats in a small sitting room that was serving as a closet, he ushered us through double doors into a hall filled with people. The band was just taking a break, and everyone was touching their glasses to gold-plated fountains that were flowing with champagne. I saw uniformed men and women offering hors d'oeuvres and heard lots of raised voices and laughing. It was quite a successful party.

"Please excuse me," Rialto said, "while I find Stella to let her know you are here." Then he vanished into the crowd.

Bill said, "Champagne?"

We made our way to one of the tables and picked up fluted crystal glasses, which we tilted into the cascade of sparkling liquid. Then we edged our way through the guests to the opposite end of the room where French doors opened onto a large balcony. We didn't go outside — it was much too cold for that — but we tried to peer through the reflections of the party in the glass to see what the view was outside. It seemed we were overlooking a river, which I assumed to be the Severn. Across the river was mostly darkness, with just a few distant lights twinkling in the darkness.

It was almost impossible for us to talk, so Bill and I smiled at each other, sipped our champagne, and continued to stare out the windows. I jumped when someone grabbed my elbow. It was Rialto, and next to him was a woman whose hair was the color of the champagne we were sipping, with skin paler than a ghost's. Her eyes had just enough blue to create color. She wore a thin white cashmere sweater over a white cashmere skirt which emphasized the smallest of curves in her hips. Rialto introduced us to his "darling Stella." The touch of her hand was ice cold, but I shook it warmly and said I was happy to meet her.

Bill gave her a hug, which she tolerated, and Rialto put his muscular arm across her thin shoulders.

"I was admiring the view," I said, indicating the French doors. "That's the Severn down there, right?"

"Yes," said Rialto, "and do you know what lies directly across the river from this house I have built?"

I shook my head "no."

"The Romanov mansion," he shouted, "Where my great-great-grandfather was murdered!"

Bill was obviously wrong about Rialto's desire not to talk about his family, but he was on target with his excitability.

"Darling, I am so tired of hearing about your great-great-grandfather," Stella murmured. "I am going to wish we never built this house."

"You are right, my Starlight. I've had too much champagne already. Do you dance, Miss Emily?"

"Yes. Do you?"

"When the band starts up again, I claim the first dance. And, Bill, you'll dance with Stella."

"Of course," Bill grinned. "I would love nothing better."

Then Rialto and Stella wandered off, leaving me a little breathless.

The band had obviously stopped for quick refreshment and began taking up their instruments again. Rialto and Stella were nowhere in sight. I was glad.

The first song of the new set was "Old Time Rock 'n Roll," a Bob Seger classic and one of my favorites. Bill and I started dancing. I love to dance and was pleased to see Bill enjoyed it also. We got brave with each other and tried out different steps. I would pony and he would do the same, then he would Watusi and I would copy him. We traded dance steps back and forth for the rest of the song, and I laughed with joy at the fun I was having. And then the lights went out.

We were plunged into darkness. *Y2K*, I thought, *the worst has happened*. I heard a door bang and felt a sudden rush of cold air. A woman screamed.

Bill said, "I'm right here," and I felt his hand on my arm. Then I heard the voice again, singing louder this time:

Darcie Malone, Darcie Malone,
Darcie, why don't you come home.

I shivered. Bill drew me closer to him.

"Did you hear that?" I whispered.

"That woman scream? Sure."

"Not that, the man singing."

"No, I didn't hear any men singing."

There were men's and women's voices talking now, people murmuring in the dark. Then there was the whoop and thrum of a generator coming to life and, suddenly, the lights were on again. We were all half-blinded by their brilliance. Bill stepped away from me. I blinked, and I thought with dismay *He didn't hear it.* It was only me. The singing was only for me. I felt nauseous and frightened. Why was I being singled out for this experience? I wanted to leave, but I didn't want to spoil Bill's evening.

"I need to sit down," I said.

We made our way to the side of the room and a small table with chairs. The band had not resumed, and I welcomed the lull.

"Can you find me some hot coffee or tea?" I asked Bill. I was still chilled although the air had warmed, and I presumed the open door had been closed.

"Of course," he said and walked off. I was shaken by the voice of Darcie's father and the knowledge that no one had heard it but me. I needed to sit and think about the implications.

But that was not to be. Our hostess, Stella, appeared with two young men dressed in casual attire and looking more like workmen than party guests.

"I'm so sorry about the lights," she said. "But the generator's on now. We'll be fine."

"Is it Y2K?" I asked. "Is power out everywhere?"

"Oh no, dear! Rialto checked. We just had some kind of electrical glitch. But everything's working now. Are you okay?"

"I'm fine. I was just spooked by the momentary blackout."

"Funny you should use that word, 'spooked.' I was just coming to introduce you to these two gentlemen who have their own business, the Severn River Basin Paranormal Society. Bill told me you were researching Darcie."

The men came forward now and gave their names: James Willis and Greg Lowe. They even had a business card, which they handed to me.

"I'll leave you all alone to talk," Stella said and disappeared into the crowd.

"I'm not sure I'm ready to do any serious investigating," I told them. "I'm a little skeptical of what people call the paranormal and those who claim to be psychics."

"We are too." James said. "In fact, when we do an investigation, we're looking first to *debunk* stories of ghosts and poltergeists. Sometimes what people are hearing are loose pipes banging against a wall. Most don't know that a fuse box leaking electricity can cause feelings of paranoia."

"Do you know the story of Darcie Malone?"

"Oh yes, everyone around here does. But no one has ever asked for our help."

"And you do this all the time? You can make a living investigating paranormal activity?

"Well, not really," Greg spoke up. "Our day job is landscaping. Ghost hunting is something we do on the side, on nights and weekends."

Bill arrived with a cup of hot tea, which I took from him gratefully. I introduced James and Greg and told Bill why Stella had arranged for us to meet them.

"Excellent," he said as he shook their hands. "When can we get started?" His eagerness to investigate a thirty-year-old mystery surprised me, but this was a night of surprises.

"Well, we need to talk about that a little," James said. "Normally we investigate strange phenomena. But in this case, there are none. In fact, that's the problem. Darcie disappeared and there are no clues to what happened. I'm not sure what Stella or you had in mind that we could do."

Bill looked at me and said, "Would you be interested in having them spend some time at the old Romanov mansion? See if they pick up anything?"

Would I! I nodded my agreement.

He turned back to the men. "Don't you do something called EVPs and video? I've read about some of your investigations online."

"Sure," Greg answered. "We could do that. EVPs are electronic voice phenomena not detectable by the human ear. We usually ask questions and see if we get a response on tape. We also use thermal imaging cameras to pick up hot spots of energy, but I think what we're more interested in here is asking questions about Darcie's disappearance and seeing if her spirit, or anyone else's, is still around to tell us what happened."

"We also have thermometers that measure changes in temperature," James added. "When a spirit is trying to manifest, it will often draw energy from the heat in the air. That's what creates the cold spots you hear about."

"Can we join you when you investigate?" I looked at Bill as I spoke to see if he wanted to be part of it.

"I'm game," he said.

"Well, we don't usually bring the client with us, but if you promise to be very quiet and walk carefully to avoid tripping over our equipment, we'll be glad to let you come along."

"Is there a charge for your services?" I asked.

"Stella assured us she and Rialto will pay for the first investigation. The others will be up to you."

"When can you get started?" Bill asked.

"Well, our families always spend New Year's Day together, so how about next Friday night? We'll go to the property around three thirty to set up our equipment before it gets dark. Why don't you join us around 6 p.m.? It will be very dark by then."

I shivered just thinking about it. "It's good for me," I said. Bill agreed.

Jim and Greg wished us a Happy New Year and wandered off, perhaps in search of other opportunities to ply their part-time trade of ghost hunting.

The rest of the evening passed uneventfully. Bill and I continued to dance for an hour or so. Two minutes before midnight the band began to play "Auld Lang Syne" and everyone took a glass of champagne. At midnight, Bill kissed me and I put my arms up and around his shoulders in an embrace. I hated to let go when it was over. I didn't want to remember how long it'd been since I'd been kissed so tenderly.

When I spoke to Janet on New Year's Day I told her, "The prince has finally arrived. A little late in life, but I'm glad to finally find him. I was beginning to have my doubts."

"Emily, grow up! Come out of your fantasy. All the real Prince Charmings are already married, have two kids in college, and a loving wife they'd never leave. You're too trusting. You must be more careful. You said he was a native, that he knew Darcie, that he was related to the Everlys. Maybe *he* killed her. Maybe he's stringing you along to see what you find out next."

The world of single, older women is a caring one. Friends watch out for each other, peering around every curve for the con man who wants to embezzle their friend's money, the serial dater who just wants fresh meat and will break their friend's heart when he tires of her in three or four months, or the pervert who's hoping for a stepchild to molest. I appreciated Janet's concern but didn't need it right now.

"He's a local, yes, but he's a reporter. He's got to have the trust of his community or he couldn't live and work here. And he's taking me to meet his family today. Don't worry." I told her. "I'll be fine."

Chapter Eleven

On New Year's Day Bill picked me up at five o'clock to go to his sister's house for dinner. *Meeting the whole family*, I thought to myself, *this is a good sign*.

His sister had a large, rambling farmhouse in the country about an hour away. During the ride, Bill gave me more family history. His sister Clare, whom I was about to meet, was the eldest. She was also a widow with two grown sons. His brother John, the restaurant owner, was the middle child and blessed with two daughters. Bill was the baby. I could have guessed this from his relaxed charm and sense of humor.

He had warned me the night before that Clare had a home full of cats and dogs, and since I am allergic to any animal with hair or fur, I had prepared appropriately with allergy medicine. He also told me she cleaned constantly, and hopefully, I would not have any problems. I hoped I wouldn't fall asleep from the antihistamines.

Like John, she was an outstanding cook, but she was a vegetarian. There would be no turkey or roast beef gracing the dining table, but there would be a selection of pasta, cheese, and salad. And although she was strict about what she ate, she was a little more liberal about what she drank. I could look forward to more than one excellent bottle of wine.

We walked into a home already filled with family and friends, and boisterous conversations about the coming election: Al Gore versus a limited choice of qualified Republican opponents. Bill pointed out Clare, a tall thin woman with vibrant brunette hair wearing a bright yellow blouse and flowered skirt. She was arguing with two men in their thirties, apparently about the Middle East. She was passionately preaching that we needed to get out yesterday, and the two men, who looked like brothers, were urging a slower disengagement.

"Give it a rest, Clare," Bill interrupted, "and come meet Emily."

She immediately stopped arguing and came to greet us. "I've heard so much about you," she said. "And all good," she added with a smile.

"I love your farmhouse," I said. "The countryside is so beautiful. How long have you lived here?"

"Since before the boys were born. That's them," she said, and the men joined us. She introduced them as Thomas and Robert They in turn pointed out their wives in the crowd.

Bill also pointed out John and his wife, Bernice, sitting on a sofa talking to two girls whom I assumed were their daughters.

"The rest are friends and friends of friends of friends," Clare explained. "I love to start the New Year off with a party."

"Thank you so much for inviting me," I said.

"Bill insisted," she answered. "And, of course, I love company."

Bill and I made the rounds and he introduced me to everyone, even though I forgot most of their names a moment later. I had no idea which nephew was Robert and which Thomas, likewise with John and Bernice's daughters Carol and Jill, but I wasn't worried. Everyone was friendly and eager to talk.

Around the dinner table, where I enjoyed fettuccini alfredo while Bill had vegetarian lasagna, the talk turned to Bill's job at the *Sentinel*. Everyone wanted to know if he was investigating anything or anybody. It seemed he had won an award or two in the past for unearthing corruption in the county government.

"No big assignments right now, but Emily is looking into the Darcie Malone disappearance thirty years ago."

Richard's wife, Laverne, looked immediately alarmed. "Please don't do that," she said, putting down her fork and looking directly at me.

"Why not?" I asked.

"I don't know, but I got such a chill just now."

"Laverne's psychic," her husband said. "She knew my dad died before the police called."

"There's a draft from the front door," Bill said. "Clare, you need to get your boys to put up more weather stripping."

Richard frowned at Bill's dismissal of his wife's talent.

Bill caught it and said, "I don't doubt Laverne has psychic abilities, but there was a logical explanation for her chill. Remember, I was there when she told Clare to get a mammogram, and it turned out she had cancer."

"In remission now," Clare assured everyone.

A woman sitting next to her whose name I had forgotten turned and gave Clare a hug. "For ten years now," the woman informed us.

"I'm so glad," I said. "I have so many friends with family members who have survived cancer. It's wonderful that there is so much help available."

"The best medicine was my family and my friends," Clare said. "Let's drink a toast to them." She held up her half-empty wine glass and announced, "To the New Year and cherished friends and family!"

We all clinked glasses and drank, then moved on to more pleasant topics.

I would have loved to ask Laverne about Walter and Darcie, but it was for the family to broach the subject and not me. As they didn't say anything more about it, neither did I.

While Bill was driving me home later that night, I told him how much I enjoyed his family. "They're such a warm, loving group. You're very lucky."

"And your family?"

"I've lost my parents and one brother. I have a sister and two more brothers back in Delaware. I'll visit them in the spring. Maybe you'd like to join me?"

"I can't wait."

CHAPTER TWELVE

Friday was unusually warm, which for New Hampshire in January meant daytime highs in the fifties going down to the thirties at night. The weatherman explained it was due to the cloud cover keeping the warm air close to the earth. The shortened days and cloudy skies were gloomy, a perfect setting for our adventure that night.

The news at work was as gloomy as the skies. By nine thirty I'd read and responded to the twenty odd emails I'm greeted with every morning. They usually ranged from customer complaints about credit declines to requests for backup documentation for approvals. At 9:35 a.m., I was called into Roger's office. I entered to find the customer service supervisor, Joan D'Angelo, already there.

"Please sit down, Emily," Roger said.

I took the chair next to Joan—a dark wood number with only a thin cushion, designed to make the occasional visitor to Roger's office squirm in discomfort. A nice reinforcement to the discomfort Roger would always be happy to dole out.

"We're moving quickly on the merger with Metrobank, and we're sending you and Joan to Concord for training in Metrobank products and systems. While their credit card products have similar parameters to ours, their systems are more up-to-date, and we'll be using their systems here as of February first. I'll need you both to learn how to use them and then return here to help implement them.

"Emily, it'll be your job to train our current customer service staff, and Joan can be your backup. It's a three-week course, and Metro will pay for you to stay at a hotel convenient to the Metro office park. I've already ordered Metro corporate cards for you both for traveling expenses. Can you be ready to leave Monday?"

I was shocked at the suddenness, but other than the ghost hunters and seeing Bill, I had no real plans. Joan looked very disgruntled, though. I believe she was married and had a small child.

I replied that I could be ready by then and asked if we were driving or taking the train.

"I'll drive," Joan spoke up. "That way I can go home on the weekends."

"Anything else we should know before we go?" I asked.

"Well, besides it being a three-week course—and you're free to travel home on the weekends if you like—I should tell you that some of the systems you'll be learning are brand-new, even to Metrobank. In fact, the customer service representatives at the Concord site will be attending classes with you. The weeks that you're going to be there, they've scheduled half of the second shift, so your class will be three thirty to midnight. Is that a problem?"

Oh my god, was that a problem! Not that I could say so, but I'm a morning person, up at 5 a.m. and in bed by 9 p.m. By three o'clock in the afternoon I'm nodding at my desk. But I needed this job. I would do anything to keep this job. I said to Roger, "No problem."

"I'll give you more details as I get them," he said by way of dismissal. Joan and I rose to leave.

"Have you ever done any business travel?" Joan asked me as we wandered back to our desks.

"Yes, but not overnight."

I was feeling a little shell-shocked. I didn't relish the hours, and the other problem was my friends Janet and Sue from my old home town of Wilmington, Delaware. Like me they worked during the day, so we talked in the evenings. I still missed them, even though it'd been ten years since I moved away.

Unlike me they had husbands and children who kept them busy on Saturday and Sunday. Weekday evenings were our only chance to talk, usually after eight when the kids were in bed. I'd have to go three weeks without talking to them, three weeks without swapping news and jokes and hearing their loving support. Three weeks of total loneliness. I was going to be miserable.

Chapter Thirteen

I left work early feigning a migraine and met Bill at my house. From there, we went to the Romanov mansion where the Severn River Basin Paranormal Society was already stringing long extension cords from the generators in their vans into the house and around the grounds. Everyone wore black parkas and thick rubber boots to protect against the cold and damp. They carried flashlights, tape recorders, and complicated-looking night vision cameras. I was impressed by their professionalism. This was not a bunch of fraternity guys having fun in the dark. This was a serious business.

James and Greg greeted us. Greg noticed our own warm clothing and said, "Glad to see you dressed appropriately. We're ready if you are. Please be careful not to trip over any of the wires."

As it was already dark, he handed us penlight flashlights and told us to follow him. We would slowly walk around the outside of the house while his crew investigated the inside. If they thought it was safe to go in, we would enter later.

James showed me an EMF detector, EMF standing for electronic magnetic field. It was like a sideways video camera that transmitted electromagnetic findings in different colors. Blue and green shapes indicated an object giving off a small amount of energy. The colors progressed from yellow, then orange, then red for more intense readings. Living things and/or spirit apparitions would glow red and orange, while furniture, structures, and rocks would be blue and green.

There were cameramen, too, videotaping the investigators. They were our silent shadows, following our every step from a distance of about six feet. The purpose was to capture movement that the investigators themselves might not have seen.

Bill and I followed James around the grounds, picking up

only shadowy images of the house, the trees, the bushes, and the snow. We were very quiet, Bill and I not saying anything, while James directed our flashlights and explained in whispers where we were going. Greg and another team member were making a wider perimeter of the grounds, and two team members were inside the mansion. Two more members sat in one of the vans and monitored everything with laptops, which were hooked up to all the cameras and audio equipment. They had portable generators for powering up their equipment.

Occasionally you would hear someone whisper "Is there anyone here who wants to speak to us?" James told us they were giving the spirits a chance to communicate. If the ghosts of the Romanovs or of Darcie were still here, they might try to communicate with words or unusual noises.

When we had completed one full circuit, we stopped for a break. There was hot coffee in thermoses and a selection of sandwiches and cookies. Even ghost hunter debunkers had to eat.

Three o'clock to four o'clock in the morning is known by many paranormal investigators as "dead time." For some reason, rather than the traditional movie version time of midnight, this is the time when paranormal activity is most likely to occur. It's the proverbial darkest hour before dawn.

At 3 a.m., Bill and I were invited to join Greg's team, which was doing a second walk-through in the house. The first crew had decided it was safe enough if we just watched where we were going and didn't fall down the stairs in the dark. Walking around the outside of the house had not bothered me, but entering the front door filled me with dread. I had the very definite feeling that somebody, or something, did not want us there. I didn't tell anyone, though. I just clung tighter to Bill's arm.

"Will you be doing a story about this in the newspaper?" I asked in a whisper.

"Let's see what happens first."

We silently walked through the living, dining, and kitchen areas, including a butler's pantry and a mudroom at the back. Nothing moved, no breeze blew, no spirit whispered in the dark. The house was silent—and very cold.

We returned to the front hall and climbed the stairs. There were four bedrooms. The walk-through of the first three was uneventful. When we got to the fourth and largest bedroom at the back of the house, it seemed darker than the others, and colder. I began to feel nauseous. Bill put his arm around my shoulders as if sensing my discomfort. I wondered if my nausea was caused by our vision being limited to only the bobbing lights of our tiny flashlights.

I became aware of a sense of evil, a sense of something dark and unkind lingering in this space. I shivered and thought about asking Bill to take me out. Then a second investigator with a night vision camera whispered, "Here's the bed where Amanda and the gardener were murdered."

I looked at his viewfinder. The bed had a burnished brass frame and the sheets still lay there tucked around the mattress, stained with huge blotches of blood, looking dark and ominous in the pale violet glow of the camera screen. The old quilted coverlet was crumpled at the foot of the bed, probably where it had been pushed by the feet of the passionate lovers. I felt colder still and more ill. Suddenly the quilt moved.

I stared at the viewfinder. Bill nudged me and I squeezed his arm tighter. No one said a word but I could feel the stillness and concentration in the room. As we stared at the camera screen, an unseen hand pulled the quilt slowly up over the sheets, as if covering up the evidence of what had happened there.

"Who's here?" James asked out loud. "Tell us what happened."

The quilt stopped moving about two-thirds of the way across the mattress, just enough to cover the blood stains. Then there was a loud bang from across the room, like a door blowing open. A cold wind blew out of nowhere and enveloped us briefly. I was swathed in a sense of evil. Then our flashlights went out, and even the pale glow of the camera was gone. "All our batteries just died," someone said.

I threw my arms around Bill and buried my head in his shoulder. I shivered and choked down vomit. I was paralyzed with panic. What dark energy was in this room? What would it do next?

Bill whispered in my ear, "We'll be alright. I can just make out the crew. They'll help us."

As if on cue James asked, "Are you guys okay? We've gotten someone's attention. I want to find the balcony."

Then the cameras and flashlights miraculously came back on and my stomach settled just a little. Bill and I, still clutching each other, followed the crew past the bed and toward what could now be seen as dim light coming in from the French doors across the room.

"Keep your camera focused on the bed," James instructed one man. Another followed the group across the room. James rattled the handles of the balcony doors but they appeared to be locked tight. "Aren't these the doors that just blew open?" he asked.

"I thought so," someone answered.

James tried them some more, but he couldn't get the handles to turn. "Guess they don't want us out there," he said. "It probably wouldn't have been safe anyway. I just wanted to get a look. Let's head back downstairs."

I thought that was a good idea.

Nothing else happened while we were there, not that I wanted anything else to happen. Bill and I stood outside a while longer as Greg walked the grounds with the tape recorder and asked questions of the night. "Are you here, Darcie? Can you tell us what happened the night you disappeared?"

At 6 a.m., as the first streaks of dawn appeared in the eastern sky, the investigation was called to a halt and the crew began collecting all its equipment.

James and Greg came over to Bill and me and asked us what we thought.

"It was so strange in that bedroom, seeing that quilt move," I said. "Do you have it on video?"

"We sure do," Greg answered. "It'll take us a few weeks to review all the evidence we collected here tonight, but we'll be in touch to arrange a time to go over what we've found."

"Well, thank you so much," I said. "I can't wait."

"Yes, thank you," Bill added. "I'm sure everyone's tired and ready to go home."

Bill and I returned to his car and drove to my house in silence. I think we were both overwhelmed with what we'd just witnessed. I'd been badly frightened. I'd never really been a big believer in ghosts or the paranormal previous to hearing the plaintive words of Mr. Malone's lonely plea. Now I had a lot of questions, not to mention a few fears of what could possibly happen after death.

As we pulled up to my little bungalow and the sun appeared just enough to illuminate the snow-covered landscape with pink and gold, I turned to Bill and said, "Why don't you stay for a while. I'm tired, but I'm not ready to be alone with my thoughts."

He kissed me gently. "I thought you'd never ask."

CHAPTER FOURTEEN

It's so wonderful to wake up on a cold, snowy Saturday with a warm, loving man in your bed. I couldn't believe my good fortune. While Bill lay sleeping, I washed away the previous day's makeup from my face and found some cozy old jeans and a soft sweatshirt to wear as I fixed us a late breakfast.

The aroma of coffee woke him, and he sat sleepy eyed and smiling at my kitchen table while I fixed eggs and toast. It was already past noon. In the few hours of daylight we had left, we planned to shovel the recent snow on my walk and then watch a movie. We talked a little about our experiences at the Romanov mansion and the incident in the bedroom.

"Do you think we were visited by a ghost?" I asked. "How else do you explain that quilt moving?"

"Could have been a residual haunting," he said. James and Greg had explained how sometimes an activity could repeat itself over and over again, independent of anyone being around to witness it. Footsteps often turned out to be residual hauntings, as opposed to what were called "intelligent" hauntings where spirits were trying to interact with the investigators.

We had seen footage of another investigation with James sitting in a chair and speaking to an entity, requesting it to rap three times or rap in a particular pattern. The spirit would respond with the requested number or pattern of raps, and respond again and again to the same request. It was all caught on tape as evidence of paranormal activity.

"And what about the wind blowing the French doors open and then locking them shut?"

"Well, that could really have just been the wind, and the velocity of the blast actually jammed the locks so that they couldn't be reopened."

"I suppose so," I conceded. "But something certainly seemed to be trying to scare us."

It was true that James and Greg billed themselves primarily as debunkers, looking for rational explanations for seemingly irrational activities. But I didn't remember their coming up with any explanation for the quilt moving on the bed.

Then Bill and I moved on to more mundane topics such as which movies to watch after the sidewalk was shoveled and which brand of microwave popcorn had more natural tasting butter.

Later, I broached the subject of my impending three weeks of travel for Metrobank.

"I'm going to hate it," I told him and elaborated on all the reasons why.

He seemed curiously unsympathetic, but pleased that I'd be returning with Joan on Saturday mornings.

"Call me when you get in next Saturday," he said and then changed the topic back to movies.

Altogether it was a very enjoyable weekend. I hoped it would be the first of many.

Chapter Fifteen

Joan picked me up at ten thirty Monday morning. She had a car that was fast becoming popular, a huge Ford Expedition. It could hold a whole Girl Scout troop and camping supplies for a week. I enjoyed sitting high up on the wide leather seats.

I didn't know Joan well, and we were silent most of the two-hour trip to Concord. Our one conversation started with my moaning about the late class hours. Joan immediately disagreed.

"I love to stay up late," she assured me. "And I love to sleep until noon. This trip will be a breeze for me."

Well, I guessed I'd better shut up. She'd probably be my new boss when we returned.

I always love the ride along Route 202 that winds through the trees and tiny hamlets of southern New Hampshire. Even in winter, with a sugar-coated frosting of snow, the bare woods are beautiful. This day, the pines in between the hardwoods were deep green and sprinkled with white powder. The sky was a blue canvas backdrop to God's magical mystery of trees and sun and snow.

Concord is well-named. It always makes me think of concrete, which is the overwhelming choice of building material for its homes and businesses. Our hotel was a drab structure of yellowing stucco and tinted windows. My room was a mausoleum of burgundy walls, burgundy drapes, burgundy carpet, and burgundy flowered bedspread. With the dark windows, not a stray sunbeam could survive. The decor couldn't be more depressing if it tried.

Joan and I unpacked her SUV, and I glanced in surprise at what she'd brought. While I had one medium-sized suitcase and a vanity case, Joan had one large suitcase and three department-store-size shopping bags of food. I saw chips, cookies, pretzels, two-liter bottles of soda, and Tupperware containers hiding indeterminate goodies. Was she not planning to go out to restaurants? Was I to be eating by myself too? Then she said, "Meet you in the lobby at one o'clock. We'll find a good spot for lunch."

The one consolation prize for business travel is eating out. Being a barely proficient cook whose mother had dusted the stove, I was at home in any American restaurant. Joan and I decided that our main meal would be in the early afternoon before class. We found a charming Italian restaurant with few cars in the parking lot. Their Veal Parmigianino was perfect. We indulged in dessert. So far, so good.

Conversation at this and ensuing meals usually centered around Joan's successful, stockbroker husband, her amazing son who at age eight was already a soccer star, and her career, of which she was especially proud as she had only a high school diploma. She had thinly veiled scorn for my college-graduate, worker-bee status. She was what women's lib literature would describe as assertive. She was having it all and flaunting it.

Before the first class, we had to check in with Roger. However, when we got to the Metrobank office, we were grilled with all sorts of questions about our identity even though we had our ID cards from the Savings and Loan. When they finally released us, Joan made a quick call to Roger to let him know we'd arrived safely, and then we ran for the classroom, which we couldn't find down any of the long hallways. Finally, a stray employee exiting the ladies room directed us to the correct corridor, and we entered the classroom breathless and ten minutes late. There were two empty seats, one in the front row and one in the back corner. Joan immediately grabbed the front row. I struggled to the back. This was not good. I was already sleepy from the large meal, and I could barely hear the instructor. This was going to be a long three weeks.

I won't bore you with all the ugly details of my getting home from class at 1:30 a.m., falling asleep around two, and waking up at five every morning despite the doom and gloom of the Concord Regency Hotel. To fill the hours till I met Joan at one for lunch, I read a ton of books, watched Regis and Kelly on TV, and completed endless *New York Times* crossword puzzles. Joan never once invited me to her room for a chat, to watch a movie, or to share her snacks.

By week's end I was seriously sleep-deprived and caught myself dozing off in class more than once. Luckily, we were given manuals to take back home with us that would hopefully make up for all I was missing in class.

On the first Friday evening, Joan insisted we drive back to Swansea after class, and I dozed off in the car. She prattled on about all we were learning, and I hoped she wasn't too offended when I didn't respond. I was too tired to care.

I stumbled through my front door at 3 a.m. and collapsed into bed, only to wake up at my usual 5 a.m. Words cannot describe how tired and depressed I was. I called Bill and explained that I was too worn out to see him that weekend. I needed the time to lay on the sofa and rest, even if I couldn't sleep. He was very nice and understanding about it, and that worried me. He made no offers to come by with takeout or a video. I briefly thought I'd lost him, but was too tired to pursue it.

Worst of all, I was too tired to arrange a meeting with our ghost hunters. It would have to wait until my three-week training course was over.

The next two weeks played out exactly the same as the first, with Joan picking me up Monday morning and depositing me back in Swansea bleary-eyed in the wee hours of Saturday morning. By the third week I had a blazing sore throat, swollen lymph glands, and pounding sinuses. I was too sick to even think about seeing a doctor in Concord; I just lived on Mucinex® and Advil® and concentrated on getting through class each night.

On the last Friday night, I somehow managed to pass the final test, and we were mercifully let out of class at 8 p.m. I was home by eleven and asleep in five seconds. At eight the next morning, I was on the phone to the GP on call and, by noon, had a prescription for an antibiotic. I miraculously managed a two-hour nap. The ordeal was over. I had survived. Never would I ever allow myself to be roped into an evening training class again.

Chapter Sixteen

The following Wednesday Bill called me at work to say the ghost hunters had reviewed all their evidence and wanted to share it with us. Was I free that night? We could grab some dinner at TGI Fridays first and then we would meet them at Bill's. I hadn't seen Bill's home yet, so I was doubly looking forward to it. I knew he had an old farmhouse where Elm Street met Route 9, and I was very curious to see how he lived. I was thinking manly leather couches and dark wood furniture, maybe a wide-screen TV, and half-dozen video game gadgets. Hoping we might resume our relationship, I was interested to know if I could make myself at home there.

Bill picked me up as soon as I arrived home and kissed me with great appreciation. Then he helped me into his car and off we went for healthy salads for dinner and sinful cheesecake for dessert.

After dinner, we drove down Elm Street to Bill's home and I was surprised to see how small it was, just a bungalow like my own, really. It had white wood siding with black shutters. In the eerie light of a lone street lamp, its lines were blurred with the surrounding snow and shadowy shrubbery.

There were no outside lights on, so we stood in darkness while Bill unlocked the front door and fumbled to find the light switch. Even before the lights, though, I was assaulted by the smell of garbage—sour milk, old coffee grounds, and that odd aroma that I've always associated with bugs.

When the lights blazed on I couldn't help myself. Out of my mouth before I could stop it came the moan "Oh no!" Bill looked at me quizzically. I was suddenly speechless.

Everywhere, and I mean everywhere, were piles upon piles of "stuff." There were mountains of newspapers, some yellowed with age; towers of shoe boxes, some half-open and spewing cards and unopened mail; mounds of clothing, some still in cellophane packages; and more piles of items it was too dark to discern.

These things were stacked up about four to five feet high and shoved close together higgledy-piggledy with narrow pathways arranged to lead from the front door to the sofa and then again past the sofa to the staircase. Another narrow path headed toward the back of the house where I supposed the kitchen was, but I had no desire to see it. I wondered how many and what types of bugs were burrowed in the twists of this trash-filled maze.

Worst of all, interspersed with the shoe boxes and newspapers were groupings of videotapes with titles like *Voyeurs of Vegas, Free and Easy in England*, and the beguiling *Dolls of Dresden*. Yuck! I felt dirty just standing there.

You can't imagine my shock at this clutter and filth belonging to such a neatly groomed, clean smelling, educated man. And almost as bad as the clutter were the walls, once white but now a weary tan-streaked with grease and dust. In its own way, Bill's house was every bit as terrifying as the Romanov mansion, with even more personal connotations. I had slept with this man, was dreaming of marrying this man, but I could never live with all the monstrous habits that his home implied. What was I going to do now?

"What's the matter?" Bill asked, seeing the stricken look on my face.

I couldn't believe he couldn't tell. Struggling to say something not too offensive I blurted out, "Don't you ever paint?"

"I've been too busy," he replied icily.

Then out of nowhere there was a rustle of...something. I couldn't place it. I hoped it wasn't a rat. Then I heard "Squawk!" I'm ashamed to admit that I screamed.

Bill burst out laughing.

"That's Ahab," he explained, pointing to a large bird perched in a dull silver cage off to one side of the dining area. I hadn't noticed it in the dim light and stuff on the floor.

I have to admit the bird was beautiful—about three foot tall with a large black beak, yellow coloring in wide stripes below his eyes, and feathers that were a brilliant aqua-shading-to teal at their tips.

"You never mentioned owning a parrot," I accused him. I dislike pet birds for no particular reason. Maybe it's the cage, or the smell, or having seen Hitchcock's *The Birds.*

"It's not a parrot; it's a macaw. Notice the black beak. That's how you can tell."

The bird squawked again. It sounded like "mal tour nay, mal tour nay."

"What's he saying?" I asked.

"You have a dirty mind."

"No, I don't, and what does that have to do with what the bird is saying?" I was seriously annoyed by this point.

"No, no," he explained. "He's saying 'mal tourné.' That's French for 'dirty mind.' It's my little joke for when I have lady friends over."

Yeah, and I'm suddenly realizing why this guy is single.

Then we heard the ghost hunters' van arrive, and I looked around quickly for a TV set. Luckily Bill did have one, a wall-mounted widescreen that easily cost in the thousands, and there was a small clearing on the coffee table among the empty Styrofoam food containers where the investigators could set up their laptop.

It was just James and Greg who arrived, and they seemed not to notice the disarray of Bill's home. They greeted us warmly while Bill moved the food cartons from the coffee table to the floor. Then Bill moved some coats and snow gear off the couch so we could all squeeze on.

James spoke first. "As you know," he said, "we always come in looking to debunk stories of paranormal activity. We make sure loose pipes aren't banging against a wall or there's a fuse box leaking electricity. However, sometimes we can't find any scientific explanations, and what we're left with we consider paranormal. Now I know we all had personal experiences that night at the Romanov mansion. That was a pretty intense one we shared upstairs in the master bedroom. But it turns out that there was even more going on, things we didn't see but caught on tape." With that, he opened a program on his laptop that contained the recordings from the audiotapes.

"Let me set the scene for you," he said. "This was recorded when the first crew went upstairs and was walking in the master bedroom. They didn't have the experience we had, but they did get something. Our tech manager, Phil, asked if there was anyone present who wanted to communicate with us. He didn't hear a response. He asked again with a slightly different wording, and still, he didn't hear anything. Then he asked a third time. He never heard anything, but the tape recorder picked up something in response to all three requests."

James touched the mouse and we heard the scratchy sounds of the audiotape and Phil's voice clearly asking if there was anyone present. Then, muffled under the static, came a female voice.

"Can you tell what she's saying?" James asked. I couldn't quite make it out. Let me play some more."

There was a pause and Phil made his request again, and again a faint female voice could be heard responding.

"It's a woman saying 'love me,'" Bill said.

We listened to Phil make his third request, and the voice came through a little stronger and clearer. It was definitely a young woman's voice repeating "love me." I felt chills travel up and down my spine.

"Do you think that was Amanda or Darcie?" I asked.

"We don't know. Because it was picked up in the bedroom, we're guessing Amanda. We picked up something else outside too. Let me play it for you."

James fast-forwarded quite a bit, and then we heard Greg outside, the crunch of his footsteps loud in the snow, as he asked "Is Darcie here? Does anyone know what happened to Darcie?"

Then we heard a soft voice, muffled in the static. The investigators played it over and over, and after a while you could make out a woman's voice moaning "no, Al, no."

"Oh my god, did he kill her?" I asked.

"We can't make that assumption," Bill said. "There are lots of things that could have been happening to which she might say no."

"But he was there. He has to have been there," I insisted.

"We have another piece to play for you," James continued.

He fast-forwarded the tape again, then paused it. "This is Melinda investigating the grounds out back where the police found the remains of a fire. The police speculated that the fire was built by Walter and Darcie the night they were there. The coals were still warm when the police got there the next morning after finding Walter."

He started the tape again, and we heard more footsteps crunching through the snow and frozen grass. "Are you here, Darcie?" Melinda was asking. "Is Darcie here or anyone who wants to speak to us?"

Then we heard a deep male voice and all it said was "Sorry."

And after each question, the same response, "Sorry."

I was stunned. First of all, I couldn't believe they had actually caught voices. How could entities without corporeal form speak and be recorded? And we were being told that Albert had been there. This was huge. What did he know? What had he done?

Next, James played the videotape of the quilt being pulled over the sheets.

"There is no way that there was anything or anyone in the vicinity that could have caused that to happen," Greg explained. "There were no wires or electrical cords on the bed, and you can clearly see that no one is in there.

"This place is definitely haunted," Bill said.

"We're not done yet," Greg interjected. "We have one more video to run for you. We had a camera aimed at the balcony where Mr. Romanov is said to have hung himself. Now, we had a lot of problems with this camera. There seem to be long stretches where it's not picking up anything, not even shapes we know are there. Then, around three thirty, we get this..."

He hit the "forward" button and the back of the house appeared, seeming to come out of a dark mist, and then was sharply outlined against the night sky. On the balcony is a dark form, not a shadow that can be seen through, but a solid shape looming over the railing and seeming to look down at the yard below.

I felt cold and nauseated, wondering if this was a ghost or a demon, maybe a spirit or a devil, claiming ownership of the house and grounds.

"What is that?" I whispered.

"We don't know," James said. "But keep watching."

Judging from its relationship to the balcony railing, the form appeared to be about six foot tall and, maybe, two foot wide at the middle. Its form was round at the top, and then sloped downward to where shoulders might be if it were a person wearing a black sheet.

After a moment, it glided back to the French doors, then glided to the railing again, repeating the motion of looking over and down as if checking out the people moving below. Then it glided back to French doors again and seemed to disappear through them into the bedroom.

"My god!" I breathed. "Do you think Darcie and Walter saw that? Do you think it did something to Darcie? Do you think that's what made Walter crazy?"

"It makes sense," said Greg, "but we can't know for sure."

"And Albert was there too," Bill added.

"There's certainly paranormal activity," Greg responded. "Now, whether this is a residual or an intelligent haunting we can't be sure. The movement of the quilt and the voices could all be repeating themselves over and over again, trapped in time, rather than interactive responses to our questions. We'll try to come back and investigate again when the weather is warmer."

I was feeling pretty paranormal myself at the moment. Between the bursting of my bubble over my dream man Bill and the voice telling us that Albert was there that night, I didn't know what to think. I didn't know what was real and what was not real. Was there anyone or anything I could trust?

"Is that everything?" I asked weakly.

"One more thing," Greg said, "And you can take it for whatever value you personally want to place on it. Melinda considers herself to be a psychic investigator. She has only been with our staff a few months, and James and I are still not entirely convinced she has this power. But she told us that she felt very strongly that Darcie was still there."

I couldn't help myself. I looked at Greg in shock and surprise.

"If she's still there, she'd have to be dead," I said.

"Yes, I think you're right," Greg agreed.

"But that's another investigation. We'll save that for next time."

Greg handed me a slip of paper with Melinda's name and phone number. "Melinda said she'd be glad to talk to you some more about it, so here's her number. Give her a call. I gather she thought you two had a lot in common."

Being as I hadn't made any women friends yet in Swansea, and my men friends never lasted, I thought I *would* call her. Maybe we'd have lunch. Maybe there was more she picked up on that she wanted to tell me in private.

James and Greg were packing up their laptop and putting on their jackets. Bill and I both thanked them, and they said the appreciation was all theirs, that it had been a fruitful investigation and that they'd be in touch. I watched them leave with a sinking feeling. What would I do now?

"I'm tired, Bill. Would you mind driving me home? There is so much I need to think about."

"No problem. I need to sit down and write up something for the paper. I hope the news doesn't upset the Malone family."

"You're going to tell them what Melinda thinks? Don't you need proof?"

"This isn't that kind of article. I'll label it as speculation. But those voices and that video, they're for real, and as far as I can figure they exonerate Walter."

I could see why that was important to him. He wanted to clear the name of his relative.

I felt awful. What kind of pain would this news story inflict on Mrs. Malone? I hadn't really thought through what Bill's involvement would mean in this case. I'd considered him a resource, not someone who would profit journalistically from my investigation. What had I done? Had I used Bill? Had he used me? I wanted to go home and pull the covers over my head, and after Bill let me off with just a quick kiss, that's exactly what I did.

Chapter Seventeen

I didn't hear from Bill the next day, and that was fine with me. I didn't hear from him Saturday either, which did surprise me but also enlightened me to his true purpose in dating me. Yes, I had been interested in him somewhat for what he could tell me about Darcie and her family, but I had been attracted to him before I knew what he did for a living. And now, as I watched my hopes for Prince Charming fade into nothingness, the realization of my own stupidity made me ache with shame. Janet was right—I really needed to grow up.

If I believed in karma, I would know that this is meant to happen and I shouldn't be discouraged or depressed. But karma is not a warm, loving man to keep me company on cold, lonely nights and empty weekends. Karma is cold consolation.

Then there was the matter of Albert. What did he know? What had he done? And how could I find out? But to answer my questions I would have to do to him what Bill had just done to me: gain his confidence, get what I was after, and then dismiss him. I couldn't do that. I wasn't that kind of person. I sat on my sofa with an afghan wrapped around me and mourned the loss of Bill, and the mess I'd made of my search for Darcie Malone.

I took time that weekend to read up on psychics and paranormal occurrences. It seems that modern science, and in particular medical science, has completely ignored one third of what makes a human what he or she is.

The human being is a delicate interdependence of mind, body, and emotions. In fact, our emotions are how our mind communicates with our body. When we are afraid, our eyes widen and we might get a tightening of the muscles in our stomach. When we are sad, we cry. When we are happy, we laugh. When we worry, we frown. But because we can't reach out and touch the emotion itself, we tend to ignore the fact that an emotion has an energy and existence all its own that often binds itself to physical objects or a physical place such as a house or car or a photograph.

Psychics are people with the ability to detect emotions and the activity they engender long after the physical body has left the scene. But like any other talent, such as musical ability or an aptitude for numbers, it needs to be developed. Reliable psychics have patiently developed their talent over time and can focus it where it's needed.

A good example would be the way a smell can linger in the air for days or weeks. You can't see an odor, or touch it, but your sense of smell will pick out an odor in the air. Sometimes the smell of fried onions in my home will seek out a corner on the second floor where I'll detect it days later. So, think of emotions like a smell—positive emotions being good smells and negative emotions bad smells. A psychic has a hyperdeveloped sense of smell and can detect odors most of us can't.

It seems like a lot of mumbo jumbo voodoo nonsense to those who don't understand it, but there's a lot of scientific evidence gathered by police departments all over the country where a psychic has pinpointed a criminal or found a body, and there is no other explanation for it.

I say all this because I decided to believe what Melinda said, that Darcie was somewhere in or near the Romanov mansion.

The article about the Severn River Basin Paranormal Society's investigation of the Romanov mansion appeared in the *Sussex Sentinel* the following Sunday. It retold the story of Isaac Romanov, Amanda, and the gardener, and then included the story of the thirty-years-missing Darcie Malone. My part was relegated to that of a "good friend" who had accompanied Bill on the night of the investigation. No mention was made of my hearing Mr. Malone singing out for his daughter, and no conclusions were drawn, but Bill did mention Melinda's speculation that Darcie was still on the grounds. Bill didn't endorse it. He left it for the readers themselves to decide what to believe. He made no mention of his family's relationship to Walter. Bill got his story, and I guessed he would probably be promoted to Features Editor. I wasn't bothered that

I was treated so shabbily in Bill's article, but I was concerned that the story might have upset Mrs. Malone.

On my lunch hour from work on Monday, I stopped by the hardware store to speak to Albert and ask if his mother was alright. My stomach churned and my head ached at the thought of causing her any discomfort, but I needed to acknowledge it and find out how she was.

In the ten years I had been in Swansea, I'd never been in its lone hardware store. Picture hooks, light bulbs, or even a screwdriver could be bought at the grocery store. From the looks of the dust and the dim lightning, I wasn't the only resident that had overlooked Albert's business. There were rows of drawers full of hundreds of different-sized nails and screws, a display of outdoor house numbers that looked ancient, and a sad attempt to attractively display clay pots and metal spades for spring flower gardens. I wondered at a man of Albert's age and intelligence molding away like damp leaves in a building where the sun never shone. Did he suffer from depression, or was he just lazy?

I followed the dark, narrow entrance row to the back of the store, where Albert stood behind a counter with his eyes focused downward, probably examining something. When he looked up, he didn't change his frown as he observed me walking closer. I could feel sweat trickling down my armpits and on the insides of my thighs. This was going to be awful.

"Hi," I offered with a nervous smile.

"You don't know the trouble you've caused me," he replied sourly. He was still frowning.

"Is your mom okay? Did the story in the paper upset her?"

"Mom?" he asked, like he hadn't even thought about her. "Why would mom be upset?"

I could have slugged him. What kind of dolt was he? That story would have upset me if I'd been her. "I just thought it might have triggered a lot of sad memories," I said.

"And you didn't do that the first day you came knocking at our door?"

"She said she wanted to talk about Darcie. I'm glad to hear that the newspaper story and all those ghost hunters didn't bother her."

"Well, to be honest," Albert said, "I'm the one who picks the paper up off the sidewalk in the morning, and when I saw the story, I threw the paper in my car and told my mother the paper boy must have forgotten us that morning. She never pursued it. I'm hoping she still doesn't know about it. Were you planning another visit to tell her?"

"Oh no. It didn't turn out like I thought it would. Do you think she'll hear about it on the news or one of her friends will mention it to her?" This was feeling very awkward. I couldn't tell if Albert was mad or just being sarcastic.

"Mom's outlived all her friends, and she doesn't go outside and talk to the neighbors. I think it was too trivial to make the radio or television news—too fantastical. So, I think she's safe. It's the phone calls to me that have me angry with you."

"Who's called you?"

"Doug Smith wanting to reiterate that he knows nothing about Darcie's disappearance, but if she is found, he'd like to have a memorial service for her. And Butch Larson, out of god knows where, called also to say he knows nothing about it, adding not to tell his wife he called. Seems he owes her a bunch of money. And then half a dozen of Darcie's old girlfriends have called wanting to know if I knew anything that hadn't been put in the article. It's been real fun keeping mom away from answering the phone. I finally disconnected it and put it in a drawer until this blows over."

"Did you know that the reporter's mother's last name is Everly?"

"Doesn't everyone? Or at least everyone who grew up here."

That was a potshot at my ignorance. "Don't you think it's odd those men called you," I asked, "when their only alibi was that they were drinking with each other at the other end of town?"

"Look, the police went into all that thirty years ago. I wasn't happy with never finding out what happened, but what else was there to do?"

"I'm sorry, Albert. I've caused you and your mother a lot of pain and heartache. I just wanted to see if I could make something happen, maybe find a clue to the reason your sister went missing."

"I understand that," he said in a less harsh tone. "And you did give me an idea. I have a feeling you're not about to let this go, even now, so why don't I introduce you to the detective who oversaw the investigation of Darcie's disappearance? He's still alive and kicking—every evening down at the Crucifixion Bar and Grill. Want to stop by there with me this evening when you're done work?"

"Now why didn't Bill think to talk to him? If this town is as small as you say, I would have thought Bill would have gone looking for him and added his opinion to the story."

"Maybe Bill had good reason not to be interested in what the police thought. Did he tell you he was a suspect too?"

"No," I said casually, but inside I was thinking *Oh, my God! I've spent time alone with that man!* For just a moment, I was almost thankful he hadn't called. Janet and Sue had been right to be alarmed.

"Come by the store when you're done at the bank," Albert added. "I'll take you to meet Bud O'Doul.

Chapter Eighteen

When I arrived back at my job, Joan was waiting for me.

"Roger wants to see us," she said. "It's time to make use of what we learned in Concord."

We sat on the same uncomfortable chairs on the other side of the desk, as Roger outlined his plan to start training our customer service reps the following Monday.

"We're under the gun to get this accomplished as soon as possible," he said. "We plan to start taking calls for Metro products at the beginning of next month. I'd like classes to start next Monday." I nodded my head in agreement. I needed only a few days to prepare the materials.

"I've discussed this with Joan, and she's feeling pretty confident that she can train also, so my plan is to have two classes running at the same time, one in the morning from 6:30 a.m. to 3 p.m., and one in the evening from 3:30 p.m. to midnight. Joan has graciously agreed to take the morning class, so that leaves the evening class for you, Emily."

What! No! Oh, my God this was the most awful news. I couldn't go through that again, not even with sleeping, or rather not sleeping, in my own house. But Joan was management and I wasn't. I was too horrified to protest.

What hurt the most was having heard Joan talk on and on about how she was a night owl, how she loved to stay up and sleep late. She knew how I struggled with no sleep and getting ill when we were in Concord. How could she stab me in the back like this? Had she lied to me? What were her motives?

I stumbled out of Roger's office with my heart pounding and my brain on fire. I couldn't do this. No way was I going to do this. Three more weeks of sleeplessness, three more weeks cut off from phone conversations with my friends, three more weeks of feeling too ill to go out on the weekends and continue my investigation of Darcie Malone. And it might not be three weeks; there might be more training needed. Three weeks could turn into six or nine or even twelve. Job or no job, I couldn't do it.

I sat at my desk for a few minutes, and then I went to see Joan.

"I need to talk to you, in private," I said.

"Okay, let's go in the conference room."

We sat across from each other, the dark mahogany of the tabletop gleaming in between us, my heart pounding like I was contemplating jumping off a bridge, which in a way I was.

"I can't do it, Joan. I can't train the evening shift. That schedule made me sick in Concord — you remember. I just can't do it again. If it means I'm fired, then I'm fired. But I know I'll be ill, and I just won't do it."

Joan's face lost all expression. Her skin tone went gray, then became hard as stone. She was quiet for ten seconds, which is a long time when you're waiting for a response.

"Metro has invested too much money in your training to throw it away," she finally said. "I'll take the evening class and you can do the morning. But don't ever, ever ask me for a favor again. Understood?"

"I understand. Thank you."

She got up and left without another word. I heaved a huge sigh of relief. I was going to be let go sooner or later now for sure, but I didn't care. I was just grateful I wouldn't be training the evening class. Going forward, I'd knock myself out and try to work my way back into Joan's good graces.

At five thirty, I was back at the hardware store, waiting patiently as Albert locked up. Since the store was on High Street up around Eighth, we were only a few blocks from the bar, and we decided to walk. I told Albert about walking into Doug Smith's car when I'd attempted to go there a few months before. He didn't comment on the Reverend Douglas Smith.

We walked in companionable silence down High Street, the early February night air cold against our faces. The town had kept their old-fashioned street lights, which gave out just enough light to see our way along the brick sidewalk. When we made the turn from High onto Third in the direction of the bar, the wind kicked up again. *Miserable place,* I thought, *even Mother Nature doesn't like it.*

The Crucifixion Bar and Grill still had its red neon cross glowing in the window. The lower façade was brick, the upper stone, with dark windows that neither let in light nor illuminated the patrons inside.

Few people want to escape the slings and arrows of outrageous fortune in a bar lit up brighter than high noon and sparkling with cleanliness and order. No, when our demons are assaulting us on all sides, whether they be the boss or the spouse or our own regrettable past, we want a place where lights are low, details are blurred, and we are enveloped in a haze of anonymity. The Crucifixion Bar and Grill was that place for the good, and the not-so-good, folks of Swansea, New Hampshire.

Albert held open the heavy wood door, and I walked into semidarkness. Off to the side were dim lights and voices. I traversed a short vestibule to a doorway on the left. Once there, I caught sight of a dingy bar, and hundreds of bottles backlit in blue on the wall behind the service area.

A beefy bald guy in a black tee was wiping out glasses while conversing with three or four men seated there. Scattered about the room at linoleum-topped tables were two or three couples whose features I couldn't make out in the haze of dust and long-departed dreams. The jukebox was playing Johnny Cash's "I Walk the Line."

"Let's sit at the bar," Albert whispered and led the way to a line of empty stools. Feeling out of place in a business suit and heels, I nevertheless climbed aboard the stool next to Albert. I chose the stool that was closest to the door.

The bartender wandered over, and I noticed a broken nose that had healed crookedly and darting brown eyes. "Don't see you in here much, Al," he said.

"Not much of drinker, am I," Albert said, "but tonight I feel like a Molson's."

"And for your lady friend?" he said with a blank nod in my direction.

"A glass of pinot grigio, please," I said.

The bartender suddenly chuckled. "If it's wine you're wanting, we got two kinds, red or white. Take your pick."

I felt chastised for assuming they had a wine cellar. "Make it white." Who knew what it would be, a hauntingly tart apple wine or a distinctively bitter two-week-old chardonnay?

As the bartender got our drinks — Albert's a beer in a frosty mug and mine, something yellowish in a scratched brandy snifter — Albert surveyed the clientele. A few stools to Albert's left were three men who had the ruddy faces and gruff voices of seasoned drunks. Two had beers and the third a Martini, dirty, with a large olive. He spoke up loudly to the bartender, "A little stingy with the vodka tonight, are we?"

"That's your fourth, Bud. I want you to get home okay."

"Home to what? My dog? He don't mind if I'm drunk."

"Yeah, but I do. I'm not losing my license over your sorry ass stumbling down the street."

"Okay, okay, but make me one more for the road."

"That's our man," Albert whispered in my ear. "Grab your drink."

I did as I was told, and we wandered over in Bud's direction.

"If it ain't old Al," Bud acknowledged him with a lift of his martini glass in Albert's direction.

"Who's your friend?"

"Emily Menotti. She's the 'friend' Bill wrote about in his story yesterday." Albert obviously felt there was no need to explain *which* story.

"Pleased to meet you," Bud said and offered me a beefy palm to shake, which I did. Now that I was closer I could see he was a huge man, with bulging blue eyes and wild white hair. He was attractive in an Ernest Hemingway sort of way. He looked like a man who had spent a good deal of time fishing in rough seas and stormy weather.

"Emily's researching Darcie's disappearance, and I thought you were just the man for her to talk to," Albert offered. "I told her you oversaw the investigation back in the day." "Just a pup myself in those days," he said. "Let's grab a table where we can be comfortable."

I carried my glass of not-too-bad-tasting wine over to a corner table that was round and had a clean tablecloth. We three sat around it, and Bud hoisted his martini glass. "To Darcie," he said, looking cautiously at Albert. "May she someday rest in peace."

"Here, here," said Albert and took a swig of his Molson's. I nodded and sipped my wine.

"What can you share with Emily?" Albert asked. "I'm assuming you've read in the newspaper all that's happened with the ghost hunters at the mansion and the psychic who says Darcie is still there. What do you think?"

"I think I agree with the psychic. I've given it a lot of thought over the years. If Darcie had run away, she would have come back by now. Your sister was basically a good girl. She wouldn't have wanted to cause your parents any pain."

"Thank you," Albert said, "for having a good opinion of her. God knows enough people thought it was a ruse to explain her leaving to have a baby or an abortion."

"But we still don't know what happened, do we? I see only a couple of possibilities, and I'm afraid they all include her death whether accidental or intentional. I rather lean toward accidental as we could never establish a motive for anyone wanting her dead. Sure, there was some jealousy. Butch and Doug would have liked to date her—or whatever passed for dating with those guys." Bud smiled. The sexual innuendo was obvious.

"And then you have their girlfriends who wouldn't have liked the competition," he continued. "And then again, there's you, Al. Everyone knew you didn't like Darcie dating Walter."

"He was a flake, Bud. Would you have wanted your sister dating him?" To Albert's credit his words weren't angry, only passionate. "If she'd got pregnant and they had married, she would have ended up with *two* kids—a baby and an ineffective husband."

"I understand, Al, but it's the old Romeo and Juliet scenario. The more you tell a teenager *not* to see a person, the more attractive that person becomes. You didn't help any making your feelings so well-known."

"I just couldn't stand back and watch her throw her life away."

How many parents had echoed these same words when faced with the same dilemma? Somehow, no matter which path you took, it always ended badly.

"In the final analysis, Bud, with your years of police detective experience, what do you think happened?" I asked.

"Well, let's review the little bit of evidence we have. We have a picnic basket with half-eaten cheese, crackers, apples, grapes, some melted ice, and an empty pint of Southern Comfort. We've got their clothes, so we know at some point they were naked. We know they were boyfriend and girlfriend. You can't deny that sex probably happened, as much as it pains you, Al."

"I've accepted that," he muttered.

"Something we didn't publish at the time, along with the clothes, we found a Ouija® board."

"What! You never told my parents or me about that."

"No, but you knew and we all knew that Darcie claimed she was going to try to contact the spirits of Isaac and Amanda and help them, as they say, 'cross over.' Those who believe in that sort of thing would have thought a Ouija® board would facilitate that. Now I can't tell you anything about the spirit world hocus-pocus, but my experience tells me they had sex, and maybe it got a little rough and out of hand, and maybe Darcie died during it. A young flakey kid like Walter might have been unable to deal with it. He might have buried her body someplace we never found, or maybe he threw her in the river. We searched that place thoroughly, but we couldn't dig up every square inch. I'm thinking she was thrown in the river to cover up a situation young Walter wasn't mentally strong enough to handle."

"But Doug and Butch and their girlfriends went skinny-dipping that night. Wouldn't they have heard something?" I asked.

"If they did they never told the authorities. And we questioned those guys plenty of times."

"Well, I'd like to talk to them about it," I said.

"This is still my investigation. You'll have to take me with you."

"And me too," Albert said.

"No, I don't think that would be smart," I told Albert. "You're too close to Darcie. They'd be afraid of upsetting you or giving you the tiniest reason to persecute them."

"When are we going?" Bud asked and gave me a wink.

Well, given my precarious position at the bank, I couldn't see asking time off from work. "Saturday morning, ten o'clock," I suggested. "Are you free?"

"I'm free for you, hon. Let's talk to Celia first. Her health is bad and she might be the most vulnerable."

"Should I call her first and tell her we're coming?"

"How many police shows have you seen, darlin'? Obviously, none. We cops never announce ourselves. We just show up and see what happens." Bud handed me a business card. "Just call me Saturday morning when you're up and ready to go."

I promised I would and got up to leave. Bud rose too. "Can I offer you a ride?"

"No thanks, I live very close. I can walk."

"Believe me," he replied. "We all know where you live."

Chapter Nineteen

On Saturday morning, Bud and I walked up the path to the red brick duplex where Doug and Celia resided. The bricks that held the ancient building together were old and crumbling at the corners. The white paint around the windows was peeling and cracked. The windows themselves were curtained and closed off to the outside world. The house looked as if it were asleep and didn't want to be disturbed.

Bud jabbed the black buzzer by the door.

There was a thunder of padded feet echoing down the inside hallway and the excited bark of a large dog on the other side the door. After a moment, the door was opened by a thin, pale woman in her late forties with limp brown hair laced with gray. It hung amazingly long, all the way down to her waist, but rather than sleek and glowing with health, it was brittle and flyaway in the cold, dry air. Above her high forehead, it was parted severely in the middle, and several broken off gray hairs stood up jaggedly and caught the light.

Large, frightened brown eyes took us in, and her voice was a mere croak as she asked, "Yes?" A large collie stood beside her, tongue lolling out in excitement over the visitors, but obediently staying still.

"Hi, Celia, it's Bud. You remember me, right?" He held out a large paw of his own for shaking. Celia didn't seem to notice. Her eyes were staring at Bud's face with a quizzical squint as if trying to recall who he was.

"This is Emily Menotti," he added. "Are you busy? Could we take a few moments of your time to talk a little?"

She stood back from the door and pulled it with her to allow us to enter. The hall behind her was full of shadows although sunlight seemed to be escaping from a room on the left.

"Come sit in the living room," she said. "I'm afraid it's a mess. I can't seem to find the time or energy to clean it up. It's very embarrassing when parishioners stop by."

"Oh, we don't mind, Celia. You're looking good. How have you and Doug been?"

"'Bout the same. Doug is busy with the church. I haven't been feeling too well, you know; the chemo drugs really do a job on me."

Bud hadn't filled me in on these details, but Celia was obviously in sad shape. She was worn and tired looking, and there seemed to be fear lurking behind her eyes. She wore a man's flannel shirt over a red turtleneck sweater. Her jeans were the pale blue of multiple washings, and the bottoms were frayed above her puffy red slippers.

Bud and I sat on a dirty green couch covered with dog hair. Celia seated herself in a beautiful wooden rocking chair with an etched headrest and gracefully carved arms — clearly a cherished antique.

"Would you like some tea?" she offered. "I seem to drink tea all day long. It keeps me awake. I have hot water heating on the stove right now."

"I'd love some," I said.

"Make that two," said Bud.

"Be right back," she replied, getting up and shuffling into the hall.

"Cancer?" I asked Bud. "You never mentioned anything about that. Is she okay?"

"She was diagnosed about ten or fifteen years ago. It went into remission. I'm guessing it's come back."

"How awful."

"I imagine she takes a pretty strong cocktail of drugs, so she probably can't drive or hold a job. Considering how little money Doug's church takes in, I don't know how they survive, maybe on food stamps and disability."

"Poor thing," I said. It was one of those situations you wanted to file away for the days you were feeling sorry for yourself. No matter how much I disliked my coworkers or hated living alone, I was still incredibly fortunate.

"Makes you think how lucky you are," I commented.

"I agree."

"Do you think she'll talk to us about Darcie?"

"Well, she seems to be fairly alert today, and she let us come in. That's a good sign."

We heard a tinkling of china cups coming from the kitchen, so we stopped talking. In a few moments Celia reappeared with a tray laden with a teapot, three cups, a sugar bowl, and a milk pitcher. She set it all down on top of a large seaman's chest that served as a coffee table. I imagined pale embroidered quilts and feather pillows locked away within.

"Here we are," she said graciously, and you could see in that brief glimpse of upwardly curved lips and smiling eyes the beautiful woman she once was and might still be again under better circumstances.

After we had spent a few minutes fixing our tea to our taste— I like at least two heaping teaspoons of sugar while Bud preferred his unsweetened but with a touch of milk—Bud thoughtfully stirred the contents of his cup and began.

"Emily has been researching the disappearance of Darcie Malone. Since you went to high school with her, I thought you might be able to tell Emily a little bit about her."

"Oh!" Celia startled and nearly dropped her teacup. "Why would you want to do something like that?" She stared at me as if I had suddenly starting sprouting horns or warts or something equally loathsome.

I decided she was trustworthy, maybe because of her illness or her frightened-child eyes, so I told her the whole story beginning with the dream and the old man singing Darcie's name, what happened at Rialto's home on New Year's Eve, and even the ghost hunting expedition. As I spoke, she grew paler and paler.

"I've heard him too. Doug says it's just the drugs I take, but I never thought so. It's too real. I know its Darcie's dad. I know his voice. It happens every year around the anniversary of the... incident."

I thought "incident" was an interesting choice of words. "What do you think happened to her?" I asked.

Celia started to cry.

Bud got up and stood by the rocker. He put his arm around her shoulders to comfort her. "I'm sorry if this upsets you. We didn't want to, but it's a mystery that's never been solved. I was hoping that over the years you might have remembered something."

"I will never forget that night, ever," she whispered.

"You and Doug were drinking with Butch and Laurie, weren't you? Did you see anything or hear anything?"

"No one's ever asked me point-blank before. No one paid any attention to me when it happened. You and the other cops just spoke to Doug and Butch. You never questioned Laurie and me. Why didn't you question us?"

"I don't know," Bud stumbled. "Those were different times. We spoke to the guys and figured if you were with them your stories would be the same. And we really didn't have any reason not to believe Doug and Butch."

"You should have spoken to Laurie and me. You should have..." Her tone was that of a stubborn child insisting on getting her way.

"Is there something else you would have told us?" Bud asked.

"Maybe...but nothing that would solve it. And I promised my husband I'd never tell. I can't break my promise."

"Celia, maybe we could make some suggestions, and you could just nod your head if we're getting warm."

"Maybe...but what if Doug finds out? He might leave me. He might disappear like Butch has. I couldn't live without Doug. I need him. I can't risk losing him."

I looked at Bud. What to do? She was so close to talking, to telling us something we didn't know.

"Maybe you could just tell us what *you* did," I suggested. Where *you* went, what *you* saw, and not mention if Doug was there or not. Just keep it in the first person singular. Then you wouldn't be telling on Doug."

Bud looked at me with quizzical eyebrows. We both knew this wasn't true. I also felt a little guilty. Were we taking advantage of Celia because she was taking a lot of drugs and maybe not in full control of her faculties? It also occurred to me that maybe she needed to make her peace with Darcie before she succumbed to cancer. I felt torn; we were so close!

"Doug is a man of God," I prompted. "What would God want you to do?"

Celia lowered her head until her eyes were inches from her chest. I could see tears falling into the teacup she held in her lap. Neither Bud nor I said anything for a few seconds while she quietly wept. Then she began:

"I was at the bar, the Crucifixion Bar and Grill, the night it happened." She spoke slowly, stopping before each pronoun to make sure she kept it in the first person.

"I was drinking beer, even though I wasn't of legal age. The bar often served us if they thought the police weren't watching.

"It was a warm evening and I heard from the others in the bar about Darcie's plan for a picnic. Walter wanted to be alone with Darcie, but Darcie wanted to see if she could communicate with the spirits of Amanda and her husband and the gardener who was killed. She thought she had psychic powers. She thought she could tell them to stop haunting the mansion and cross into the light.

"Someone...in the bar suggested that it would be fun to dress up as ghosts and scare them. We would go to the second floor and make moaning noises and let Darcie think she was speaking to the ghosts. It would be so funny to fool her, and maybe scare her a little too.

"So...someone...got some sheets and went out to the old Romanov mansion. We parked a few blocks away and snuck up on it so no one would hear us. Then we...I...went inside, went upstairs, and put on the sheets.

"I snuck out onto the balcony, crouching down to keep from being seen. I could hear Darcie and Walter below. I thought it was funny that they were naked. Darcie was speaking to the spirits, telling them to 'go toward the light.' She was so serious. Then...I... began rocking back and forth, making moaning noises."

Here, Celia lowered her voice and began swaying back and forth in her chair.

"Darcie...we're sorry...we don't want to go..." Celia spoke in a low, singsong voice that sounded truly creepy.

I imagined the teenaged Darcie hearing voices in the night. How frightening that would be.

"What did she do when she heard you?" I asked.

"She totally believed us. I was so surprised. So, we...I...kept up the moaning and the rocking. She seemed excited that she had actually contacted the dead spirits of Amanda and her husband and the gardener. She was looking up at us on the balcony and saying, 'go to the light, go to the light.'

"Then I started to get cold, real cold. I was shivering. I was starting to get scared myself. Then I felt the hair on my arms stand up, and I had this feeling of dread, of hate, of someone telling us we didn't belong there. I turned and tried to leave the balcony, but a sudden wind came up and blew the door to the bedroom closed. It was a huge, loud, ear-shattering slam! The cold intensified and blackness seemed to come down over me. I couldn't see the stars or the moon or my friends. I heard a woman scream, and I truly didn't know if it was me or Laurie or Darcie.

"I began crying and shouting 'no, no, leave us alone.' I didn't know what the black thing was or what it was dong there, but it felt evil. I thought I was going to die."

Celia stopped here, and I noticed she was trembling. Her story was a match for my own experience, only I had been inside, not outside on the balcony. Bud didn't say anything. We waited for Celia to compose herself.

The collie came up to her and offered his head to be petted. She obliged, and it seemed to calm her down. After a few strokes she looked up at us and continued.

"This is the hard part, the part I don't want to say...When the blackness lifted away from us, I heard more screaming, but this time it was a man screaming. I could tell it was coming from down on the ground. I could tell it was Walter. We...I...looked over the balcony and he was standing there, naked, screaming to the sky. He looked up and saw us and started screaming louder. He was pulling his hair and slapping himself in the face, telling himself to wake up, it was all a bad dream. At his feet lay Darcie, not moving.

"We...I...tried the balcony door again and it opened. We thought we should go before we were discovered. When we got downstairs we saw Albert arriving in his car. We didn't want him to see us. We waited in the house until he got out of his car and started walking around to the back. Then we ran like crazy and got in Butch's car and drove away."

Celia put her face in her hands and started crying in earnest, but she kept talking through her sobs.

"So, you see, we really don't know anything. I saw Darcie lying naked on the ground. I saw Walter naked and screaming. But I don't know what happened to her."

"You all left together and no one saw what happened to Darcie?" Bud asked.

"No, we don't know what happened." She'd abandoned the pretense of the "I" narrative. "We were all on the balcony moaning and pretending to be ghosts, and then we left."

"Okay, Celia, thank you. I won't tell Doug we spoke."

Bud rose, and I took that as my cue to stand up and leave with him.

"Can I get you anything before we leave?" he asked her.

"No, I'll be alright." She had recovered somewhat and was petting the collie again.

We let ourselves out.

CHAPTER TWENTY

"So, Albert was there. Do you think he killed Darcie?" I asked Bud as we walked back to his car.

"No. I think Darcie was already dead. I think she died of fright. But I also think we should talk to Albert. Let's ride over to the hardware store."

Bud had a sporty red Acura TSX into which he had to carefully lower his large body. He must have really loved that car to put up with the difficulty of getting in and out.

"You didn't tell me about your experiences with old man Malone singing Darcie's name," he said as he drove. "Funny that Celia had the same experience."

"But no one else that we know of," I said, not wanting to reveal Mrs. Malone's secret. "It's odd. What are you going to say to Albert?"

"I'll just tell him what Celia told us and see how he reacts."

"Sounds like a plan," I replied and grinned stupidly. I was enjoying this big guy and his little car, and we were getting closer to solving the mystery of Darcie Malone.

When we got to the hardware store, Albert didn't look surprised to see us. We waited while he rang up a customer, and when the customer left, he locked the front door and turned the CLOSED sign around.

"Let's sit in the office," he said.

We went to the back of the store and behind a counter to a narrow door that led to a tiny office paneled in sixties' cheapo wood paneling and lit with a couple of dingy bulbs. Albert took a seat behind a gray metal desk, and Bud and I settled into metal folding chairs on the other side.

"What did Celia tell you?" He got right to the point.

Bud explained, "Well, she said she, Doug, Butch, and Laurie went up to the old mansion that night. They put on sheets and went out onto the balcony to scare Darcie and Walter. They were, moving around and moaning, pretending to be ghosts. Seems like they did a pretty good job of it too. She said they looked down from the balcony and saw Walter naked and screaming in fright, and they saw Darcie lying naked on the ground not moving. They got scared and high-tailed it out of there, but not before they saw you arrive. Looks to me like you weren't being truthful back then, and now either. I think you better tell us what happened next."

Albert sat there thoughtfully. His hands were clasped together, but he kept nervously opening his palms and then closing them again, making this weird noise almost like a farting sound. Soon, tears started forming on his lower eyelids, and then they were spilling down his cheeks.

"I didn't know about those guys dressing up as ghosts. That explains a lot. She was dead when I got there." Then he added, "I didn't think you'd believe me."

"Do you know how she died?" Bud asked.

"She looked like she died of fright. Her eyes were huge and her mouth was wide-open as if she had died midscream. I thought maybe she did see a ghost. All I can tell you is the impression I got, and that was that she had been literally scared to death. It was horrible."

"What about Walter?"

"Well, Walter was screaming like a banshee and wouldn't answer any of my questions. He and Darcie were both naked, which I thought was odd at the time, but looking back I guess they had been making love or perhaps it was some weird witchy ritual for summoning spirits. I don't know. I only knew that my sister was dead, and someone was probably going to be blamed for it.

"I tried to resuscitate my sister, but it didn't do any good. Then I looked around and Walter was gone. I didn't know what to do. I couldn't just leave her like that, but I had to protect myself too. Walter had seen me. If people knew I was there I'd get blamed. Even if the police believed me, how do you explain it to your parents? 'Sorry, Mom and Dad, but she was dead when I got there'?

"When a beautiful young girl dies for no reason, someone has to take the blame. Someone has to be punished. Someone has to go to jail. I didn't think it should be me. So, I buried her in the front yard, right under a bush by the driveway. I couldn't believe you never found her."

"What were you doing there in the first place?" Bud asked.

"When I found out about the picnic from some friends, I knew they were going there to have sex. Or at least Walter was going there to have sex. I didn't want my sister getting pregnant without being married. And I didn't want her marrying Walter. I had to go there and stop it. I really don't know if they had sex before I got there or not."

"Can you show me where you buried her?"

"Of course."

"Let's go."

We three went out to Bud's Acura; I volunteered to sit in the back while Albert lowered himself into the front. We drove in silence out to the mansion.

After we pulled into the driveway and parked, Albert climbed out and pointed to a rhododendron already covered with buds for the coming spring.

"She's under here," he said.

Surprisingly, or maybe not so surprisingly since he was a detective, Bud pulled a shovel from the trunk of the car. He handed it to Albert.

"Dig," he said.

Bud and I sat quietly on the front steps of the porch as Albert attacked the bush. First, he loosened all the dirt for four feet around it, and then he began digging.

The bush was over thirty years old, so even with neglect it was a good size. Albert was no teenager, so it took him about an hour just to dig a foot down on the three sides of the bush that were not against the house. When he sat down for a breather, Bud got up and pulled a large rope from his trunk, one end of which he tied around the base of the bush, and the other around a hook in his trunk. Then he got into the car and started the engine. Ever so slowly he dragged the huge bush out of the earth along with a good six feet of tangled roots. When he killed the engine and got out of the car, he saw Albert and me sitting on the steps with horror-filled faces. There among the twisted roots remaining in the ground were short lengths of white bone peeking through the disturbed dirt. I'd finally found Darcie Malone.

Chapter Twenty-One

In the end, Bud could not keep his promise to Celia.

Not being a member of law enforcement, I didn't get invited to the meeting of the Swansea Police with Celia and Doug Smith, and Laurie and Butch Larson. They corroborated Celia's story, and no charges were filed against them.

Bud told me that there was little to be learned from Darcie's remains because they had been in the ground for so long. In the absence of any forensic clues such as cuts or scrapes to the bones, and no motive, they could not arrest anyone for her death. It was classified as accidental for lack of any evidence to the contrary.

Albert was arrested briefly for criminally disposing of a dead body and hindering an investigation; he pleaded guilty and got a suspended sentence. I spoke to him briefly on the phone and got the impression that he was glad it was all over and the truth was out.

Bud accompanied me to the memorial service for Darcie and stood by me as I spoke to Mrs. Malone, who had come in a wheelchair.

"Thank you, dear," she said. "I'm so glad we finally found her."

"I had to," I explained. "Mr. Malone would have never let me go."

"He loved her so much. I hope you were able to keep your job and that everything is going okay for you now."

How kind of her to be concerned for me. I assured her my job looked secure for the near future.

I gave Albert a hug and said good-bye. Bud drove me home.

As we were driving, Bud was silent with his own thoughts. I, meanwhile, was thinking about the events that had led me to the discovery of Darcie's body. I had understood from things people had said that my life and my investigation had been followed quietly by many of the town folk. Albert had taken me to the Romanov mansion and later to see Bud, Bill had taken me to meet Stella, who had introduced me to the ghost hunters, and Bud had taken me to Celia's home for the final revelation of what had happened that night. It was almost as if the persons involved in the story hadn't wanted to come forward on their own. They wanted someone else to do the dirty work of questioning friends and relatives, someone else to point the finger at the guilty person. They needed an outside party, and I had graciously stepped in to fill that role. They had waited thirty years for me. In the interim, they'd patiently allowed the now deceased Walter to shoulder the blame.

As I was climbing out of his beautiful little red car, Bud said, "Would you like to go out sometime? I know I'm a little older than you, but I think we'd have fun."

"I think so too. Call me."

Not Prince Charming, I thought to myself, *but still a Prince.*

THE END

QUESTIONS FOR THE AUTHOR

Is the story of Darcie Malone based on a real person?

Yes, part of the story is based on a friend's memory of his aunt disappearing around Glen Berne, Maryland. I believe it happened in the 1940s or '50s; he said she was never found. One afternoon we visited the haunted house where she and her boyfriend were the night she disappeared, and it was quite spooky. We went back again later that night, but were too frightened to go any further than the driveway.

Have you ever seen a ghost?

Unfortunately, no, I've never seen a ghost. However, I believe that most ghosts really don't care about being seen.

Have you ever had any other paranormal experiences?

I've had a few instances of *déjà vu* that were quite strong. One happened when I was nineteen and visiting Oxford, England. I believe in reincarnation, and perhaps I had a previous life there.

Turn the page for a preview of the next

Emily Menotti Mystery:

WHAT KILLED ROSIE?

CHAPTER ONE

MAY 2000

"Meet me at the Laundromat at seven thirty this evening," my neighbor, Jackie, said. "My laundry should be ready for the dryer by then. We'll have an hour to grab a bite to eat."

So, at 7:25 p.m. I left the small, white frame home that I share with my boyfriend and started down Elm Street to meet my neighbor. It was one of those soft spring nights in New Hampshire that you wish would go on forever — no harsh sun, no stinging rain, just the warm caress of the evening air.

The approach from Elm Street brings one to the rear of the Laundromat. When I was about a block away, I saw a figure emerge from the back door. She paused under the solitary bulb hanging over the entry, the only point of light in the gathering dusk of the evening.

The woman carried a plastic basket brimming with clothes. As I approached, I could see that it wasn't Jackie. This figure was older and had brownish, rather than pale blonde, hair. The woman whose features were becoming distinct looked bizarrely familiar.

She paused for a moment beneath the halo of light. When I got close enough to see her clearly, what I saw took my breath away. I was looking at my friend, Rosie, who had been dead for five years.

I started to run, half-stumbling over the broken pavement. I had to get closer; I had to find out who this person was.

Then my foot caught a wayward tree root and I fell, smashing my chin on the cement. Dazed, I pulled myself up to a sitting position. I looked for the woman in the doorway. She was gone.

I sat there for a few moments, dabbing at a bit of blood on my chin and feeling foolish for falling. When I picked myself up, I went inside the Laundromat and saw Jackie pulling her clothes from the washing machine. I asked about the woman with dark hair that I'd seen in the doorway.

"What woman?" she replied. "There's no one here but me."

Follow the clues with Emily Menotti as she unravels still more mysteries:

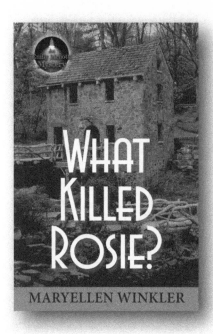

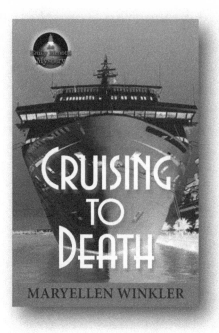

Who did Emily see in the laundromat doorway that warm May evening?

It looked like her old friend Rosie. Problem is, Rosie died of a heart attack five years ago, and now Rosie's old boyfriend is reporting strange occurrences at his condo. Is it Rosie's ghost demanding revenge? Or is someone trying to perpetuate a hoax? Join Emily as she searches among Rosie's acquaintances to find out what really killed Rosie.

Intrepid amateur sleuth, Emily Menotti, is on her first Caribbean cruise along with the Wayward Sisters book club. As they head out of New York City, however, a friend goes missing.

With the help of her clairsentient pal, Melinda, Emily starts investigating. Yet even a séance, guided by Melinda, reveals more old secrets than new clues.

Set amid tropical backdrops, this mystery has motives aplenty, including an ex-husband, a former high school boyfriend, and the on-going resentment of two unmarried friends.

Join Emily as she solves the mystery on a chilling cruise with some uninvited passengers: jealousy, revenge, and death.

Emily Menotti Mysteries are available on Amazon.com.

CPSIA information can be obtained
at www.ICGtesting.com
Printed in the USA
JSHW021853051219
2735JS00002BA/19